MW01075609

SHORTY

WILLIAM D. BRAMLETT

To my friend Katie

Love,

Dale

William D. Bramlett

This is a work of fiction. The events and incidents have been passed down through stories, some true, while others are fictitious. Names of the characters have been changed. The dialogue is a product of the author's imagination. Any resemblance to actual persons, living or dead, or actual events, is purely for the purpose of telling the story.

ISBN: 9781726868716

for:

Jimmy

Introduction:

Shorty is a fictionalized account of a real person, an authentic, uncomplicated black man who lived in the southern United States in the early twentieth century. He possessed a vitreous but unbreakable soul into which one family was allowed to see. His life taught them the absolute error of prejudice and bigotry. Hardened by the fire of man's hatred his soul over time became tempered by the desire to treat all people impartially with fairness.

Many of the stories are true as told to my siblings and me by our father years ago. My purpose is to honor the man who helped my father's family survive the Depression Years and, who I believe, is responsible for creating in our family the desire to accept those we misunderstand or believe different from ourselves in any way. Growing up in the deep south during the 1930s, northern Mississippi offered anything but a recipe for white people to tolerate, let alone respect people different from themselves.

This is not meant as an exclusive indictment against the South, or the state of Mississippi. Sadly, I have witnessed the prevalence of prejudice with its awful outcomes everywhere I have lived across America, north and south. Unfortunately, it's fair to say the South has earned the preponderance of attention on the matter. However, dislike for those different from us is not a regional problem or relegated to the confines of the borders of any particular state.

Neither is this an attempt to make excuses. The inexcusable consequences of bigotry shall remain inexcusable; the deplorable acts of hatred for fellow human beings shall remain deplorable while the unacceptable unwillingness to change shall forever be unacceptable.

Scholars argue that our advanced brain and opposing thumb put us on a higher level than other living things while religious leaders say it's our soul. An advanced brain and inherent interest in things spiritual place us as the dominant species. But, there is doubtless any question the role our childhood environment, like other creatures, plays in shaping how we think about each other. Similar to birds or mammals, what carries us through life begins with our parents. Children frequently adopt their father or mother's occupation. The poor remain poor; those educated are raised by educated people. Likewise, the seeds of our prejudices are planted in the environment of our youth, fertilized in the culture of young adulthood, and harvested as adults as all too often a bitter tasting fruit. Our social makeup comes from watching and listening, learned the same as geese following their parents across a lake.

Any likelihood of genetic predisposition to prejudice seems ludicrous. The inability to accept difference must be initially attributed to the experience of our childhood. Afterward, the subculture within which we live too easily reinforces hardened attitudes. Prejudice is the negative aspect of bias, the errant application of learned preferences. It becomes a cancer of the soul but like cancers is curable or at a minimum can be put into remission though both require considerable effort.

Unlike all other creatures, however, either our mental capacity or our spirituality or both give us the ability to make choices, thus the responsibility to act. Like the poor who pull themselves out of poverty or those from uneducated beginnings who become educated, we can, each of us, decide how to act toward others regardless of our beginnings. Embracing people culturally, racially or different in any way from us shall remain difficult, if not impossible until we recognize how we became who we are.

We must somehow look at life from behind the eyes of others, through their life lens. When we do, we will see hopes, dreams, trials, failures, joy, and sadness similar to our own. Fellow human beings live behind those eyes, each a universe unto themselves, comparable in many ways to each of us.

Until we do, all races, all cultures, all religions will continue to struggle with becoming anything close to the kind of humanity Shorty exemplified. With life experiences offering more than enough justification for bitterness toward Caucasians, he chose to become a better man. My hope is these stories portray an accurate representation of the man. The family names have been changed. Told through the eyes of my father, represented by the character of Johnny, though the majority of stories are true none of the dialogue is. But like the preponderance of history, though the actual conversations are lost, the actions live on affecting us for generations.

No apology should be required for Shorty's dialect nor for the country speak of the other characters. Neither should any of the actual people ever have to apologize. Though the reader may struggle to understand, I aim to capture northern Mississippi, at the time, more realistically.

Shorty's legacy is now my father's. My siblings and I have learned, experienced and inherited, through the culture of our family of origin, a life approach which attempts to set prejudice aside. Unfortunately, even the well-intentioned among us often fail in our efforts against this prejudice, bigotry, intolerance, unfairness, discrimination snake with many heads. The consequences of a life well lived by Shorty have filtered through to the children of my siblings and me. Without question, our country, our world, is in need of more Shorty's.

Chewalla Cemetery

I first saw him in the spring of 1933 at Daddy's funeral. Standing off to himself, he held a twisted, tattered brown felt hat low below his waist with both hands. His overalls looked a half-size too big hanging away from his chest covering a white shirt buttoned high to the neck possibly out of respect for the person being buried. Being the lone black person there, the urge to look over conflicted several times with my need to pay attention to what the preacher had to say. Everyone would expect me to stay focused on the Pastor.

Even as an eight-year-old I already had opinions about black people. They weren't favorable opinions as a result of the influence of certain members of my extended white family who spoke in disparaging terms of anyone not white. My beliefs on all matters concerning black people were, at the time, based purely on negative comments made by others. Never having spent any time around people of color to form my own beliefs, naturally the words and actions of others would do so for me. At the time I wanted to go over to find out why he had come announcing my desire for him to get away from Daddy's funeral. I was sad and I was mad. Lashing out at somebody or something might help. The unwanted outsider struck me as an appropriate target. But at least pretending to hear every word Pastor Carter said came first and foremost, standing there with all the others in the rain. Otherwise, either Mama or my big brother would tear into me.

Daddy's brothers had taken his casket up to the Chewalla Primitive Baptist church from our house earlier in the morning in an old farm wagon belonging to Daddy's Papa, Grandpa Lewis Cook. Grandpa Eddie, Mama's daddy, told me Chewalla in Indian language meant Supreme Being explaining the term Supreme Being had basically the same meaning as God. This created a certain amount of confusion raising the question of why we sent Missionaries to tell the Indians about God if they knew already. But adults did plenty of things impossible to understand. We buried Daddy in the church cemetery. A good number of other people were buried there already. The grave markers had names like Cook, Greer, Reid, Jones, and Vaughn. A Protestant cemetery for white people, there were no Catholics, no Negroes, and no Indians; though the name of the place came from some Indian God. Daddy's grave had been dug in the Cook section. Cook graves were all over the place. Close by a crumbling tombstone marked the grave of my Great Grandfather William B. Cook who fought for the

South during the Civil War. Daddy's marker would say William B. Cook too. He got the name from his Grandpa.

Proud of his name, my Grandpa Lewis told us kids on more than one occasion the importance of being mindful of our family name never doing anything to bring the Cook name disrespect. At my age, the concept of family respect hung like a lead weight around my neck because an eight-year-old could think of any number of unsavory things, which on the surface struck me as nothing more than good fun, but upon further consideration were perfect candidates to bring disrespect. Family respect ranked high on the list for the adults on both sides of my family but especially Grandpa Lewis. My siblings and I wanted to please him in all the ways a Grandpa deserves but any verbal encounter with Grandpa Lewis required successful navigation through his intimidation factor, the likes of which got the attention of everyone around him. Though not mean-spirited in the least, the thought of having to answer to the serious old man on the issue of respect frightened us.

In between the distractions of thinking about all those Cook relatives buried in the cemetery and family respect, not to mention Grandpa Lewis, my best effort was required to pay attention to the Pastor. But the time needed to listen to everything the man of God had to say far exceeded my capacity for staying in one place.

The rain had begun earlier, right before we went inside the church for the first part of the funeral. Water ran off the steep metal roof in sheets causing small rivers to form running to the back slope down a hill into Chawana Creek. Uncle Wes told us the creek's name came from another Indian word meaning crooked. To my way of thinking all creeks were crooked. Knowing they were not all named Chawana created one more thing to wonder about. Inside the church front entrance, piles of dripping umbrellas of varying sizes and colors lay about. Having never seen more than a handful of umbrellas for sale in Mr. Pearson's store at Holly Springs, a large number of them must have been bought in Memphis.

The storm boomed with heavenly claps of thunder throughout the Pastors sermon adding more fear than usual when he got to the part about us going to Hell if we didn't believe in Jesus. As he talked about Daddy being in Heaven the storm let up. Sunshine began streaming through the windows, cut by the stained glass into purples, greens, golds, and blues. The resulting multi-colored design reflecting on the cross behind the Preacher created a heavenly scene as though God himself decided to work in tandem with Pastor Carter on my daddy's behalf.

Everything had become pretty wet when we came out later to the cemetery when a slow drizzle of rain began again. Mysteriously, rain seems to accompany those sad events. At Daddy's burial, my shoes got covered in mud from the mound of dirt next to the grave meant for going back in the hole to cover the casket. A colder than usual spring day, I'm sure the wet weather made the day feel all the colder. Everybody who came got soaked standing out at the gravesite listening to the last words said by the Pastor. Continuing to preach as though he forgot to cover the obligatory matters completely inside the church, it became apparent right away Pastor Carter didn't realize the rain had started again.

The preaching, as well as the praying, seemed aimed at certain others in attendance, who in the Pastor's opinion needed saving more than dealing with how hurt we felt about Daddy's dying. Pastor Carter never missed an opportunity to save someone. Based on the kind of language often coming from my Uncle Wes, including some others not necessary to name, a few extra minutes in the rain would be time well spent if it gave any of them a chance to see Daddy again someday in heaven. Without a doubt though, having to stand there so long caused me to feel myself getting older by the minute. Looking across at Grandpa Lewis noticing the old man's wrinkled face and long ears produced visions of me standing in a rainy cemetery one day, old. My hand went to feel my ear.

But if not getting older, everyone for sure continued to get wetter. Getting into Heaven wasn't something of concern on this particular day or any other to me. Not worried in the least at the time, heck, my brothers and I were pretty much immortal. Sure, we got into pretty scary stuff once in a while, none of which could have killed us, or we didn't think so.

Most grave markers in the cemetery were for people born a long time before Daddy all the way back into the 1800s. Only a couple of graves belonged to children named Cook born around the same time as him. A larger number of gravestones showed the names of people born long before who died of old age. Except for those children, Daddy would be the youngest among all the Cooks. At thirty-two, Daddy by my way of thinking at the time was old, but Grandpa Lewis already reached seventy. He stood right there alive as any of us. Mama's daddy, my Grandpa Eddie, standing behind me, was over sixty-years-old too. Why Daddy had to die earlier in life than so many others made no sense.

Standing next to Mama with me were my brothers Junior and Wes and sister Sara. My older brother's real name wasn't Junior. Another William B. Cook, Mama called him Junior in as much as they named him the same as Daddy. There must have been people named William Cook way back in time because all our names came from a grandpa, grandma, uncle, or aunt. Wes, my younger brother, turned six in February. He had the same name as Daddy's youngest brother Uncle Wesley. Apparently, the youngest brother should always be named Wesley. Sara, fourteen-years-old in February, the oldest in our family, got her name from our Grandma Sara Cook. They named me Johnny. Daddy had an older brother named Johnny. Having the same name as him supposedly meant something. Though not having much time around Uncle Johnny myself, no one ever said anything terrible about him which put a kind of pressure on me.

Many of us being named after someone else in the family became quite confusing. When everyone got together to celebrate a holiday knowing if someone had said something to my uncle, one of my other cousins named Johnny or me could be difficult to figure out. Likewise, there were a bunch of Sara's, Wes' and William's but only one Junior. Though not a subject to spend a great deal of time on as a kid, thinking back, it's possible they felt the names were special wanting to make sure they lived on forever. Or maybe no one wanted to take the time to think of new names.

Mama hadn't said anything all day. She let Daddy's family take care of everything for the funeral. Staring a lot all morning, she sat giving up a slight smile once in a while when one of us kids went over saying something in a quiet voice or to lay a hand on her shoulder. Junior was sad enough too but worked hard at not letting his feelings show. As an eleven-year-old, in my opinion, he could do or handle about anything including Daddy dying too early. Junior defined what a big brother ought to be. Tall for his age, he was slight of build but strong. Messing with him required making sure Mama or another adult stood nearby to save me if things went badly. Messing with everybody came instinctively to me. Standing there in the cold, wet, cemetery holding Mama's hand he looked straight ahead unflinching at the casket and the hole they were putting our daddy in. My big brother never said anything about his feelings of Daddy dying or the funeral or burial. He seemed to just deal with it. There would be other times his ability to handle tough situations made a long-lasting impression on me. Those days gave me an early glimpse of a big brother who would earn my respect more than just about anyone in my lifetime.

Looking at my shoes, they had gone from light brown to dark, the thin leather soaked as if they were worn swimming in the lake. Wiggling my toes the cold water squished about squeezing out the top before running off.

Finally, the words my ears began to expect might never come but longed to hear from Pastor Carter came, “Let’s pray.”

Thankful at first this meant the preaching had ended; my initial jubilation took an unexpected setback when the prayer began to go too long. The word Amen had powerful meaning loosely defined as, ‘Phew, it’s finally over.’ My impatience being disrespectful to Daddy never occurred to me. Heck, he would have seen things the same way. If he had been standing next to me, holding my hand, he would have looked down and given me a wink. But he wasn’t standing there. Never again would he hold my hand. Daddy laid there in a wooden box barely big enough for him, going into the ground.

Mama stood with us kids next to Grandpa and Grandma Daniels. Grandpa Daniels name was Edward but adults changed it to Eddie. Grandma Daniels’ name was Mattie Lee. Grandma Mattie said the Lord must have been ready for Daddy to go. How somebody thirty-two years old could be ready to go if the Lord Himself had decided their time was up made no sense to me, especially if they were somebody’s daddy. My wildest imagination couldn’t come up with any age acceptable for dying.

My grandparents and uncles from Daddy’s side of the family stood across the grave from us.

Mama's folks never got along well with Daddy's, a mystery which would remain unsolved for a long time. Grandma Sara stood next to Grandpa Lewis. They were the Cook family. We were all Cooks. She cried all day. She either had tears running down her face or had just wiped them off with a handkerchief borrowed from Grandpa Lewis. He must've owned as many handkerchiefs as acres of land. Junior said he owned half the county, 3000 acres which is a lot, though not quite half the county.

Like a lot of the men of his generation, Grandpa Lewis didn't show any emotion except anger sometimes. The day of Daddy's funeral would be little different. But right before they lowered the casket into the ground Grandpa ambled over to the grave. Without looking at anyone, he bent down sideways resting an open palm on the rough sawn planks used to fashion the top. He patted it softly. Standing there for what seemed like forever with eyes closed, he said the things no one but a father has to impart to a dead son, the entire time patting as you would a small child on top of the head. He said Daddy shouldn't have died before him, it didn't seem right and God shouldn't have taken him so soon. Funny though, Grandpa never said he loved Daddy, but I'm sure he did.

Turning away, his head hung low, still without a word to anyone he walked out the cemetery gate alone down the hill from the church back toward his farm. Uncle Wesley took Grandma Sara by the arm escorting her from the cemetery. They caught up with Grandpa Lewis a little way down the hill where he had stopped sitting on the rim of a broken wagon wheel left beside the road. There they stood a long time in front of him holding his hat, the rain pouring down, dripping off his drenched hair onto the ground. Mama told us Grandpa and Grandma Cook never lost a child before except for one who died less than a week after being born. She said children aren't supposed to die before their parents. God's way of handling things certainly seemed different though. My sister said it wasn't some kind of rule though adults must have felt it should be. She said losing a child meant our Cook Grandparents would be sadder than everybody else. Sara's explanation made me feel bad for them though the idea of anyone else feeling worse than me seemed impossible.

After the Amen and after Grandpa Lewis walked away Daddy's brothers lowered him into the hole to begin shoveling the dirt pile. At first muddy, difficult to shovel, after removing the top layer, the gravelly, dry, dirt underneath sent up a small dust cloud with each shovel full. For the next several minutes my uncles dropped load after load into the hole. Crunching and clacking, the pebbles hit with a bounce, running along the wooden casket top before settling to a stop where they would stay buried forever with Daddy. Dust drifted up, hovering near ground level, which made seeing the casket difficult long before the dirt covered it completely.

We stood a while longer. As they continued, panic came over me as the thought occurred Daddy could still be alive in there. But after remembering how quick his arm got cold to the touch less than a minute after his breathing stopped, my concern faded. Sara stood with me next to the bed when his last few gasps of breath came. She thought we should run for help but shaking my head, no, it didn't make sense to me. The doctor said Daddy would die any day. After he endured such pain for months no part of me wanted something else done to keep him lying around hurting any longer.

But what concerned me more at the moment was never seeing him again while at the same time, leaving him in an awful cold hole in the ground. We were doing exactly that, leaving him in the ground forever with a bunch of Cook's he may never have known. Except for those dead people, Daddy would be all alone in the rain in a dark hole covered by a huge pile of muddy dirt.

As my uncles continued their shoveling, my gaze wandered over once more to the black fellow. There the uninvited stranger stood in the rain getting soaked like the rest of us, not moving, behind the short white fence which made a border between the cemetery and the rest of the churchyard. Others who were leaving the burial service walked past him turning their heads to give him a curious look. They, too, must have wondered what business the fellow had coming to William B. Cook's burial.

But this time he caught me looking. Staring right into my face he gave a slow, methodical nod in my direction. Somehow, though realizing the nod had been meant as a friendly gesture, it didn't please me in any way. Caught off guard, it caused me to look back at once to the grave which by now my uncles had nearly filled in. Thinking this fellow had interfered with our families' sad occasion made me angry adding more confusion for an eight-year-old perplexed enough after the events of the past few days. Knowing the adults standing in the rain with me also pondered unanswered questions about the untimely death of our daddy may have made me somewhat less concerned, but I doubt it.

Unwanted Intruder

Grandpa Eddie leaned over to Mama whispering something about us needing to make our way home before somebody got sick from standing too long out in the rain. Anyone who wasn't family had left including the Cook side of the family except for the brothers working to finish Daddy's grave.

Before she had a chance to respond Grandpa added, "Emilie, there is someone I want you to meet before we go." He didn't often call her Emilie, usually just Em. Mama had no other siblings. Grandpa Eddie and Grandma Mattie would do anything for her. Grandpa must have used her full name for the simple reason everything all day long had taken on such a serious tone.

"Okay but nearly everyone is gone. Besides, I think I know everybody who came. Give me just another minute," she said.

After Grandpa nodded his agreement, she said to us, "You children wait here with your grandparents."

Not knowing what she had planned, we all agreed. None of us asked why. Letting go of Junior and Wes' hands, she stepped up to the edge of the grave. My uncles stopped shoveling taking a step back with heads half-bowed. At first, she stared down at the partial mound, then up into the sky. The entire time her lips moved but no one could hear what she whispered. After looking up into the sky for a long minute, her gaze turned one final time to the grave. Placing her fingers to her lips, she kissed them lightly holding them down as if offering Daddy one last goodbye. Standing like a statue out from under the umbrella the rain began to run off her hat making a small puddle on the ground at her feet. Turning back to us she took Grandpa's hand and they began to step away from the grave. It was as if her actions had completed the funeral. The rest of us followed along without being told to.

She said, "Okay Daddy, I'm ready, who is it you wanted me to meet?"

"It's this fellow over here honey," he said pointing to the man standing at the fence. Squinting as if looking into a blinding sun, which was nowhere in sight today, with pursed lips thinking hard, this made me wonder, 'What in the world is Grandpa up to wanting Mama to meet that strange fellow.' My siblings walked close behind trying not to step in the low spots filled with rainwater around the older graves. My squishy wet toes were wrinkled as raisins. More water on them wouldn't make any difference but somebody would smack me or say something for tromping right through the enticing puddles, which should be expected of an eight-year-old in his right mind.

Avoiding the old graves altogether was a real concern though. The idea of falling through onto the bones of some distant cousin conjured up all kinds of spooky thoughts providing all the excuse necessary to stomp the water out of the puddles. Otherwise, where else could a person walk? But finding out the identity of this mysterious person including the reason Grandpa wanted Mama to meet him today of all days, concerned me more at the moment.

Grandpa stopped at the fence proceeding to introduce them, "John this is my daughter Emilie Cook. Em, I want you to meet John Ashford."

Lowering his head a little to avoid making eye contact with her he said, "I's pleased to meet you, Miss Emilie. I's so sorry bout yer man Mister William ma'am. Mister Eddie done tolt me the other day."

The Civil War ended seventy years before as did the practice of one person owning another. Well, the idea wasn't gone from everybody's mind though the result of the War along with some new laws had long since made owning someone else no longer legal. Regardless, a whole lot of people around northern Mississippi didn't believe a Negro man should look a white woman in the eye let alone offer to shake her hand. Emilie Cook didn't agree in the least, calling those white people backward, outdated and otherwise utterly ridiculous.

Staying close to Grandpa under the umbrella she extended a wet gloved hand saying, "It's nice to meet you, Mr. Ashford. And thank you for your kind words about my husband."

Looking at Grandpa Eddie first, the stranger got no sign of rebuke. Using all the caution learned over the years, he reached across the fence. Shaking the rainwater from his fingers, the fellow took Mama's hand as gentle as if he was taking a newborn baby to hold. His hands were blacker than a moonless night, large and powerful, her white glove disappearing inside. Though permission had been granted non-verbally by Grandpa, still without looking her in the eye, he held on for no longer than an instant.

Grandpa spoke again, "Em, John worked on a track gang at the railroad until a couple of weeks ago. The rail bosses fired him to give the job to a white man. Firing a man whose skin is one color to give the job to one who's a different color ain't right but it's happening everywhere right now. For now, he's staying in the old cabin on our place in exchange for him helping you out around the farm. You would need to feed him though. He's got a little money in the bank but nobody knows if the bank is going to survive or lose everybody's money like so many others have."

'Oh my gosh,' my brain raced. 'That stranger wasn't uninvited. Grandpa Eddie invited him, and he just asked a Negro to come around our farm to work right alongside Junior, Wes and me.' The day had been bad enough having to bury my daddy but now this.

Grandpa always did what he could to help others. A church deacon, any time the church organized food to help the poor he would be right in the middle of their effort no matter if the people were white or black. We were poor in those days though we had plenty of food. But there were other people close to starving. Grandpa Eddie's opinion was people shouldn't starve regardless of what color they were. At the moment though, there wasn't enough time to think. My mouth began a bad habit of taking over for my brain long before my eighth birthday.

Grabbing Mama's arm my out of control tongue blurted out, "Mama we don't need any help with our farm. And we for sure don't need help from a Negro."

An immediate excruciating pain pierced the muscle in the back part of my upper arm. Junior had grabbed a chunk of my arm pinching hard to pull me away from Mama quicker than my words could roll off my tongue. "Shut your mouth Johnny, it ain't your place to say anything about this. I'll smack you..."

Mama interrupted but stayed calm whenever my brother tried to take charge, “Junior, let him go now. And Johnny I’m not gonna have any unkind talk. You apologize to this man right this minute.”

Thinking straight became near impossible with my arm throbbing in agony. What in the world justified an apology of any kind? Wouldn’t she appreciate me saying we could do the work ourselves? Also, calling him a Negro couldn’t be the reason, the man was a Negro. But none of it made any difference. Mama had required an apology. When she required anything my reasons, regardless of how valid they might be, always went unconsidered.

Looking at the ground I muttered, “Sorry,” in a quick, quiet as possible way.

“Tell the man to his face and say it loud enough for him to hear you.” Mama would never let the matter drop which didn’t surprise me any.

Looking up his eyes met mine for the second time. Though not understanding why peering into his eyes revealed the presence of a sort of pain. If the pain came from something said or done by me, it didn’t matter to me in the least at the moment. The hurt in his eyes came from something else. Like the bad blood between my Grandpas, it would not be revealed for some time. But my own pain and anger were significant at the time causing a total disregard for anyone else. The black stranger would be the last person to get any sympathy from me.

Somehow forcing myself, my tongue spoke for my head though not my heart, “I’m sorry.”

A blink of his eyes with a slight smile changed his look. Rainwater rolled off his bald head dripping off the end of his broad brown nose.

He said, “It’s okay Mister Johnny. I knows it’s a pretty hard day for you. My pappy died too when I was near bout yer age.”

Not knowing what to say or do, after blinking a couple of times myself, continuing to look into his eyes somehow revealed honesty, kindness, caring, and a bunch of stuff difficult to understand at the time.

Mama spoke again, “I’m awful sorry to hear about your pappy Mr. Ashford. I would be happy to have you help us providing it’s no bother to you. We have plenty of extra beans and ham hocks. I can make all the cornbread you can eat.”

The situation continued to worsen. Mama had offered to feed this fellow our food. If this guy ate as much as his appearance showed we could end up without enough to eat like those people Grandpa Eddie always tried to help through the church. Mama must have been about the kindest and gentlest person ever born. Never once in my life did she say anything bad about another person, including black people. The same wasn’t true of many other people including a lot of grown women. Grandpa Lewis talked bad about black people right in front of them.

"Thank you, ma'am. I promise you won't be disappointed in me. But if it's okay with you, could you jiss call me what everybody else does? Nobody calls me Mr. Ashford ma'am."

Mama answered, "We will call you John if you prefer that to Mr. Ashford."

"Well, no ma'am, peoples don't call me John neither. They's always calls me Shorty ma'am. I never gots to be such a big man as other folks exceptin around my belt, but I promise you I'm powerful strong and a hard worker. I can do jiss bout anything I put my mind to."

Surely Junior hadn't thought this through. Trying to enlist his support for my side while holding on to my hurting arm, I silently pulled on the sleeve of his shirt. When he looked down at me shaking my head no, the frown on my face was the only communication left at my disposal. Saying anything more out loud would incur possible trouble from Mama. Junior just smiled with raised eyebrows shaking his head, yes, before turning back to watch the adults. Looking over at Sara as a possible ally would be a waste of time. The only time she would agree with me on anything is if I promised to do her chores for a month just for fun. Heck, doing her chores for a day would bore me to the point mine would be the next funeral. Little Wes was my only possible ally but no one would listen to him including myself. My cause had become hopeless in less time than it takes to pull the wings off a fly.

Mama smiled for the first time since Daddy died. A real smile too, not the ones she had given all day long to make us believe she was doing okay. "All right then, Shorty it is. Boys, Sara, this is Mr. John Ashford but we are all gonna call him Shorty."

And we did. We called him Shorty for the rest of our lives.

Indian Country

Darkness comes early when it's rainy late in the evening. Nighttime seemed to come even earlier on the day of the funeral though. Everyone was sad, or at least the people in my family. Nothing made sense as though the world had ended for everybody around me. People were sad in their own way which bewildered me since no more than one or two of them said anything to Daddy the entire time since he first got sick. He got sicker every week at first.

Every day close to the end, even though the last few weeks he lay in bed at our house, the only visitors to amount to much were our Grandparents. Grandma Sara came more than anyone. She would stay, sitting with him for hours, bringing food for all of us but always some broth or anything she could get Daddy to eat. As time went by, he ate less saying nothing tasted good to him. In the end, he couldn't have weighed much more than Mama who was tiny. Not much made me sad before, but the short period of time surrounding all the events of Daddy's death taught me a lot about the meaning of sad.

We all went back to school the next week. Maybe my thoughts were on Daddy instead of listening when Mrs. Shelby began teaching our class about the Indians who lived in the area back in the early 1800s. Who got to Holly Springs or Mississippi first didn't matter to me at the time.

Our family's story of coming here to find a better place to farm topped all other history stories about the place we called home. If the Indians were okay to leave for whatever reason God must have wanted them to, just like he wanted our family to move in. Pastor Carter would, without a doubt, sort the situation out the same way. And, if the Pastor thought God wanted us to have the land instead of the Indians, who should argue? So, whether this had been Indian Country or not in the past didn't make a lot of difference to me. Born here where my daddy was born and buried pretty much assured me of being buried here someday too.

My first year in school began as an eight-year-old. Daddy kept me home before to help with the farm chores on our place south of town. Mama kept insisting Daddy should let me go. He gave in just before the cotton harvest in the fall. Sara started school when she turned six. Daddy agreed to let Junior go when he was eight, so he had little argument to keep me out longer. Anyhow, Mrs. Shelby said the Choctaw and Chickasaw Indians lived here until our family came with others before the Civil War. She said those Indians prospered in the area for hundreds of years before a Spanish guy named Fernando Desoto with his men made their way up the Mississippi River looking for gold. Thinking the word prosper meant well to do like my Grandpa Lewis, it seemed to me that Mrs. Shelby might have her facts confused about the Indians. The only Indians we ever saw were dirt poor, evidence enough they had never prospered in the least.

Chickasaw Indians had lived in the northern part of the state while the Choctaws were south of us. Apparently, the Chickasaws were ferocious fighters which is the main reason the Spaniards didn't stay long. Not only did the Indians own slaves, but they also captured Indians from other tribes selling them as slaves too. Sometime in the early 1800s though, they agreed to move out of the area completely though a few had finagled ways to stay.

In my estimation, Mrs. Shelby was old long before the first time Johnny Cook ever laid eyes on her. She had thin, straight, gray hair like the color of a silver dollar. Her body was pretty thin too. Junior said she needed to eat at our place a lot, Mama's biscuits and gravy could fatten her up. The idea of having Mrs. Shelby at our house disturbed me though. Getting through class listening to her whiny voice all day long required every ounce of my patience. There weren't many ounces in me, to begin with. Making it through an entire evening with her for dinner could cause me to either scream out loud or else fall asleep right there at the table, or both.

The way she looked over the top of her glasses with her thin face and sharp nose reminded me of our chickens. Sometimes when taking a turn at chopping off a chicken's head for our dinner my brother held the unfortunate bird on the chopping block with me saying, "Sorry Mrs. Shelby, but we gotta eat or else we'll be as skinny as you."

Mama and Sara never saw the humor, but Junior and Daddy did. My big brother would stand right there helping to make sure my fingers didn't get chopped off at the same time. Of course, nobody hated the old woman. None of us would ever do something like chopping off her head, but sitting in school thinking about it, her running around on those skinny, chicken legs without a head, interested me a lot more than anything she tried to teach. She was so old though maybe she lived around here before the Indians which could explain how she knew so much about them.

She said, "The Spaniards had the same awful heat and humidity. They had to endure the same swarms of mosquitoes the Indians had learned to live with long before. But they also had the added weight from the heavy armor breastplates, helmets, and leggings. Illness had been an enemy worse than the Indians as Desoto's men made their way north into the Delta country. Their trip was blunted though, shortened by the difficult environment."

Picturing a blunted trip took so much thinking time her next few comments went right over my head. My understanding of blunted was like a knife with a dull point. She couldn't have meant they had a dull trip. Their escapades sounded pretty exciting except for the part about the mosquitoes. She said the Spaniards were looking for gold but also wanted to convert the Indians to Christianity. But all they succeeded in doing was to make the Indians aware of the ill treatment they would get from the white people who came along later.

Mrs. Shelby went on to emphasize we were living in Indian Country. She thought they still owned the place, not the people who lived here now. We learned about Indian wars all over the country which got me thinking if we were living in Indian Country they might come back some day which could mean lots of trouble for my family including everybody who lived around us. But I never saw an Indian on more than a couple of occasions when going into town with Daddy. The town, called Holly Springs, had been named the county seat for Marshall County, Mississippi a hundred years before in the 1830s. The courthouse on the square was the best place to see an Indian. They came to town sometimes to make a claim against property owned by a white person.

Our teacher referred to folks like my Great-Great-Grandpa and his brothers who came over from Georgia to settle here in the year 1844. She didn't mean just my folks, but she did use the term 'all' the people who moved here in those days looking for a better place than they left behind in Georgia, South Carolina, and Virginia. She said Mississippi had antediluvian soil, better for growing crops than those states they were leaving behind. Every time she used a big word like antediluvian, my immediate concern was being required to spell it. More than half the time the meanings of those big words escaped me. Spelling them could be downright terrifying.

We never heard how Mrs. Shelby got here or when, she must have had a better excuse than all those other people since she talked like they had intruded on the Chickasaws. But in 1933 there were more important things to think about than what happened to a bunch of Indians who, in my mind, had been here too long anyhow. My Great-Great-Grandpa's family didn't mean to hurt anybody by moving here. Hearing how good the soil was, they, with lots of other folks, simply planned to move out and claim a parcel. They probably didn't have any idea Mississippi had antediluvian soil.

A proud man, Great-Great-Grandpa Cook worked hard to earn his own way. The Cooks settled in Virginia in the late 1600s from Cork, Ireland.

After moving to Mississippi Great-Great-Grandpa decided to prove his trustworthiness to the men who ran the local bank. He borrowed $100 agreeing to pay the loan back within a year's time. Though informing the bank the money would be used to help get his feet on the ground financially, Great-Great-Grandpa never had any intention of buying anything with it. Instead, he put the entire $100 in a safe place to make sure every dollar would be there at the end of the year. After the note matured, he simply took the same $100, plus the $3 interest, back to the bank.

The Cook name meant everything to him. As a new man in the community, he felt it important to become trusted. The strategy worked because he ended up owning a large amount of land which got passed down to Grandpa Lewis Cook. Uncle Wesley told the Great-Great-Grandpa Cook part of our family history to Junior and me back in the winter.

Once the Chickasaws had been moved out white settlers began buying the land from the Federal Government. Cotton farming soon became big business in Mississippi. We learned in school the cotton farms were responsible for bringing in the black slaves from Carolina tobacco farms or other places including some direct from Africa. By the time our family moved here before the Civil War, there were nearly 200,000 black slaves in Mississippi. There were less white people at the time. Our state became the largest cotton-producing state in the country. Mrs. Shelby claimed all those black folks should be given credit for making our state so successful.

She wouldn't talk much about the slavery issue though except to say the Founding Fathers of the country couldn't deal with it. They left it to Abraham Lincoln and the Civil War to sort out. The impression it left me with was she had some pretty strong opinions against slavery she would not bring up. Junior said she didn't speak on the subject because some parent would complain to the school board saying she was stirring up trouble in favor of black people.

But there were lots more than 200,000 of those black folks living around our area in 1933 most of whom didn't have any way to make a living. As the cotton industry became more mechanized, there weren't many jobs left for them. Many of them moved to cities like Jackson or Memphis; some moved up north to find work while others worked as tenant farmers working land owned by white people, eking out a living before the Depression. Things had become much worse for them after the Depression began which is why Grandpa Eddie said the railroad fired the stranger he introduced to Mama. All the talk about Indians and black people being affected badly by us whites compounded itself in my mind. But with no way to make sense out of any of it, I just figured those people groups had to take care of themselves like we were taking care of ourselves. How much could we be expected to focus on their treatment or well-being as hard as things were at the time for us white people?

Sitting in class listening to Mrs. Shelby prompted me to think my family story would have been more interesting than all the stuff about Indians. The Spaniards were undeniably fascinating though. Those guys had horses, all kinds of armor and guns. A sweet old lady, Mrs. Shelby would have been better off spending more time trying to put on a few pounds than standing around all day talking about Indians. Junior was right, she was skinny.

Investigating the Stranger

As soon as school let out, I made a trip straight to Grandpa Eddie's house. My brother always walked home with me. Our older sister went to a different school, but we went by each day waiting until she got out, all of us walking home together. Knowing Mama needed Junior to move some fence posts which were too heavy for me but too light for the two of us offered an opportunity to get away from him for a little while. Otherwise, we did everything together. Informing him Grandpa Eddie wanted me to help him with something at his place didn't raise any suspicion though as usual Junior wanted more information. But in the end, he let me get away without having to make up any big lies. If my brother knew the reason for my visit with Grandpa Eddie, he would have caused trouble for sure. Junior seemed to have taken sides with the black fellow.

Grandpa Eddie and Grandma Mattie lived outside of Holly Springs on a piece of property too small for a cotton farm. They didn't need to farm anyhow. Grandpa worked as a clerk for the Frisco Railroad. The railroad ran from St. Louis all the way to Mobile, Alabama. Geography wasn't my best subject but the name Frisco referred to a big city in California. From what Grandpa Eddie said his railroad didn't go anyplace near California. Why grown-ups would come up with such a name confounded me to no end.

But my visit to Grandpa Eddie's wasn't to talk about how the railroad got its name; there was investigating to do. Finding out more about this Negro fellow coming to our place was important. Only with more information would there be any chance of talking Grandpa into changing his mind about the idea entirely. Mama's parents lived in a two-story house. Growing up there, her parents left her room unchanged with dolls on the bed, frilly curtains, and girly bed coverings. Sara spent time up there every time we visited. Wes went with her once in a while. Though there was something special about seeing the room Mama lived in as a little girl Junior and I quickly decided to find other things to do, usually outside.

We lived in a shack on our farm compared to their house. Our place had four rooms. One for eating, the kitchen, one Mama called her living room, one belonging to our parents, while the last one belonged to all four of us kids. Grandpa Eddie's house had four rooms downstairs with four more upstairs. They had a parlor in the downstairs too. Telling my friends my grandparents had a parlor made me feel richer than them in some contorted way. My friends didn't know anybody who had one. None of us realized having a parlor in no way proved they had wealth. My friends didn't know what a parlor was. Though not positive myself, the fancy room made an impression on me with a multi-colored rug from India covering the oak floor, a sofa, and two comfy stuffed chairs. On one side of the room, Grandma Mattie had a cabinet full of tiny breakable figures she never allowed anyone to touch.

An oak roll-top desk sat on the opposite side. Grandpa Eddie kept all his railroad papers stuffed into the tiny cubbyholes inside the roll-top part of the desk. Simply watching him roll the top up or down had entertainment value. A variety of hard candy in a jar had its own cubbyhole stashed up high in the desk, so little kids like Wes had to ask permission to get their hand into it. How his jar always had candy inside remained a mystery to me. But not only did he keep it well supplied he kept the best flavors like licorice, butterscotch, and green peppermint. If the big roll-top had been my desk, the candy jar would always be empty.

A Monday afternoon, Grandpa would be at home. Tuesday through Saturday was his work days at the train depot in Holly Springs. Grandma Mattie stood outside working in her garden. She always had a garden but once the Depression came everybody had one. People who didn't live on a farm would try to find a small plot of land to use, borrowing the parcel from anyone who had some extra. Grandma wore the same apron for gardening all the years we went to their house, blue with white flowers covering the pouch in front used for carrying newly picked vegetables or flowers. Though acquiring plenty of stains over time plus a little wear and tear, you could be assured her favorite apron would always be clean. Calling out to say hello I asked to make sure Grandpa hadn't gone to town or someplace though his pickup sat in its spot next to the house.

She looked up right away, "Hi Johnny, yes your Grandpa is working at his desk. You can go in but make sure you wipe those shoes off first. How's your mama doing?"

She always reminded us not to track mud in. Mama reminded us, too, whenever we were all there together. Like most things, the constant correction we got could be credited to my younger brother Wes. My guess is Grandpa Eddie never said anything about needing to wipe our feet because Grandma Mattie had to remind him too.

"Thanks, Grandma, I will. Mama's doin fine, I guess. She hasn't mentioned anything about Daddy in a couple of days, but I'm sure she thinks about him a lot."

"She will think about him for the rest of her life, but over time it will get less painful for her. It's a hard thing, losing a husband at such a young age."

Grandma must have had some knowledge to base her comments on but obviously not firsthand since Grandpa hadn't left her alone at an early age. Up the few steps a broad porch wrapped around the front extending down both sides all the way to the back. Two over-sized cane rockers sat on either side of the front door. One had a basket beside it full of Grandma's knitting. Her cat Tinker hid behind Grandma's rocker watching my every move. We never cared much for cats at our place. Tinker knew that better than my grandparents. Stopping to stare at her for a few seconds I gave a quick jerk of my head causing her to skitter around the corner of the porch to safety. Of course, if Grandma had been sitting there the scene with the cat would have played out differently. Grandpa called the cat Stinker probably to get a rise out of Grandma though he said the cat smelled bad. We kids never noticed a bad aroma but called it Stinker anyhow but only when Grandma couldn't hear us.

Next to the other chair sat a small three-legged table. A green glass ashtray with the remnants of a bit of unsmoked pipe tobacco sat on top. The round table top had notches around the outside edge which held pipes handy for Grandpa to use when taking a break from his work. They must have served him well since he took plenty of breaks.

We often saw him sitting in his rocker tapping on the pipe, digging around in a bag of tobacco or blissfully puffing away. Every time now when a whiff of pipe tobacco floats my way I'm reminded of Grandpa Eddie. Their house always looked the same which gave me a good comfortable feeling. They had left the front door opened to let the spring air come inside through the screen door.

Making a brief, polite knock, I proceeded to open the screen door calling out, "Grandpa, are you in there?"

My strategy was to go in with my best behavior to have any chance of coming away with a successful conclusion to the matter about the black man. This called for being polite about entering the house. Inside had a particular smell, though not a bad smell; not stale or moldy, more like what could be described as a 'Grandparents' aroma.' Sometimes on Sundays, the entire house smelled like cooked oil when Grandma made fried chicken. But most days her flowers created a perfume fragrance similar to cut lemons and freshly picked roses. Combined with the sweet burning tobacco from Grandpa's pipe, to me, this became the way a grandparent's house should smell. I'm sure our place had an aroma of its own too. With three boys living there, the odor would have been more of a dirty sweat smell than fresh cut flowers. Of course, it would be different if Mama and Sara lived there by themselves.

Before Grandpa could answer, I noticed him bent over the desk looking through his papers. Sitting in a cane-backed swivel chair in front of the desk with sleeves rolled up, his usual smile beamed my way. He had a great smile which could make me feel better when everything was going wrong. Thin and wispy in stature, Grandpa Daniels stood a little over six feet tall. Grandma always said he was, 'Bald as a baby's butt.'

My younger brother was the only baby whose butt ever got exposed to me, but we were too close in age for me to remember how bald his butt was. A thing like being exposed to a baby's near-bald butt is not something an eight-year-old would easily forget. Regardless, for a long time, I expected a baby might have a bit of white hair on each side of their butt cheeks like Grandpa's head. Though not a single hair on the top, he had plenty on the sides, straight and snow white. He liked keeping it long. He kept the bushy white mustache long too. A pipe placed in his mouth went in along with a bunch of mustache hairs. His mouth wasn't visible except when one of those big smiles moved the mustache up out of the way.

"Hey there Johnny Cook, I thought I heard your grandma call your name. What are you up to today? Come on in here, son."

Though we saw Grandma and him at least once a week at church we got the same greeting from him every time as if it had been years. Wanting a good spot right next to him I crossed the room stopping on the edge of the rug placing my hand on the leather covered arm of his chair. With serious questions to discuss, his ability to hear me good was a critical requirement. Sometimes he asked me to repeat things. After positioning myself strategically next to him my nerves gave in causing my first words to stumble out, off the intended subject.

"Grandpa, uh, what are you workin' on?"

His eyebrows raised making crinkles across his forehead reminding me of several rows of newly sprouting cotton seeds. With eyebrows as thick as his mustache, he bent his head down and leaned forward to look at me over the top of his glasses.

The long wait gave me the feeling at least two more birthdays could have passed before he said, "Well, I'm doing railroad paperwork. Did you come all the way over here to talk about my paperwork?"

How adults somehow sensed when something was up puzzled me. Though it wasn't my nature, if some good answer didn't come to me, I might chicken out. Junior said Cooks didn't chicken out and this wasn't the time to start.

"Actually, it's about the Negro fellow, the one from the cemetery."

Hopefully, making a non-critical statement would be a safe way to start my investigation. His eyebrows dropped, a frown replaced his smile. Crap, maybe from his point of view my comment sounded critical, even unacceptable.

"You mean those fellas who dig the graves, pretty hard job they have."

"Well, no, not those guys..."

"Oh, you mean old Samuel who keeps the grass mowed nice and low."

"No, Grandpa, holy smokes I don't mean any of those people. I'm talking about the stranger you introduced Mama to, that Shorty guy."

"Oh, Shorty, why didn't you say so? How are things working out with him at your place so far?"

He knew exactly who I wanted to talk about and probably just wanted to make me say the man's name. We provided plenty of entertainment for Grandpa often at our own expense.

"What...oh...things aren't working out at all. He hasn't even come around yet. That's what I wanted to talk to you about."

Grandpa turned to his desk laying his smoldering pipe in the ashtray. Looking back to me he said, "What is it you want to discuss son?"

His response suggested maybe he wasn't angry though the look gave me a bit of concern. But neither the response nor the look should have been a surprise. In my eight long years of living, never once had he sounded angry, though he should have on plenty of occasions.

Whenever Grandma disagreed with him on something, regardless if Grandpa should win for whatever reason, in the end, he would merely say, "Okay Mattie Lee, if that's the way you want it."

Maybe none of those were over anything serious. Grandpa would give in rather than fight about something except for serious issues. Apparently, there were few serious things in his mind. There must have been more Cook in me than Daniels since nearly anything could be considered serious enough for me to fight, not with just words either. Junior must have had more Daniels in him than Cook. My older brother would fight, but only as a last resort.

Grandpa appearing willing to have the discussion made me somewhat more comfortable getting right to the point. "Well, having a Negro around our farm all the time might not be such a good idea. What if he steals something?"

The question wasn't likely to receive a favorable answer but seemed as good a way as any to begin the negotiation. And, anyhow, maybe Grandpa hadn't considered the idea the fellow could be a thief. In reality, being a thief or not made little difference to me. My main concern was having him around at all. Placing his left hand over his mouth he silently fingered his mustache, his index finger flipping the long mustache hairs up and down, over and over. Grandpa Eddie sat for a long minute not saying anything. The mustache hair flipping occurred when any of us kids asked a hard question. Either he didn't know what to say this time or else wanted me to think on my own.

Whatever his reasoning the waiting always made me uneasy to the point of repeating the question but sometimes with a frustrated tone. "Grandpa, what if he steals from us?"

Answering right away this time, he apparently just wanted to hear the question twice. "So what do you think Shorty might steal?"

Grandpa made an excellent point to my dumb question. We didn't have anything anyone would want to steal except maybe our mule. "What about Jane, he might steal Jane?"

Grandpa sat back laughing, "And how do you think anyone is gonna steal a mule crazy enough to run right over them to get back to the barn as soon as they take one eye off her?"

His question made me stand silent. Thinking of another angle caused me to further realize brainstorming more questions beforehand would have been a good idea. My strategy had not been well thought through.

"Johnny, what's the real reason?" He leaned close to me, eyebrows raised in a questioning posture.

My arguments were going to have to get a lot more...ugly, "People say you can't trust a Negro.

Some say they don't know how to work. Besides, they're not like us."

Any sensible reasons continued to escape me leaving me standing silent again, clueless as to the best way to proceed. My reasons, including a couple of ugly ones, seemed like nothing more than bad excuses, all of which should have stayed inside my head. Maybe this is what Grandpa wanted me to figure out for myself by employing his tactic of making me wait before giving an answer.

He said, "So, people say that huh? I know what lots of people say. It's usually nothing more than repeating things they heard somebody else say. I tell you what, why don't you keep an eye on him for a while. Tell me anything your new helper does you think is not right."

His response was the best I could have hoped for. Mama's reaction at the cemetery had made the matter a foregone conclusion anyhow.

Nodding yes, all I could think to say was, "Grandpa, can I have a piece of your candy?"

After reaching for the jar he smiled pulling it back in the last second saying, "First, let me tell you some things about Shorty."

'Great, here comes one of his lectures.'

Thankfully, he never lectured as long as Pastor Carter preached or prayed. Grandpa's lectures covered a variety of subjects. Pastor Carter's preaching would be about the same topics over and over. Of course, his subjects had eternal consequences but were more difficult to remain focused on than anything Grandpa had to say.

Shrugging my shoulders while nodding in agreement again he began, "Shorty is a man just like your daddy, your uncles, Grandpa Cook or me. Well, not exactly like us. His skin is brown while ours is white, well, sort of white. But his blood is red the same as ours. He breathes the same air the same way we do and gets hungry like us."

"Yeah, I know Grandpa."

"But wait, I'm not done yet. I've seen him around other people at the railroad. I've seen him help white people who didn't think a black man should have a job there. He works with a smile on his face. He's a hard worker Johnny. They had no reason to give his job to somebody else just because he's black and the other fellow is white. But he just took off his hat politely thanking the railroad boss for giving him a chance for as long as he did. I don't know any particulars but I expect he's had a pretty hard life. Let's give him a chance. If he messes up, we'll send him down the road."

Grandpa Eddie had gone out of his way willingly to offer this black fellow a place to live for a measly promise of helping us out with our farm chores. I didn't agree with Grandpa about why Shorty got replaced by a white man. Our families were white, white people needed to work too.

But something told me firing the fellow wasn't a fair way to treat a person though figuring out why would take me a lot of hard thinking. Taking a piece of Grandpa's candy I said goodbye to Grandma and him making the four-mile walk getting home just before dark. Four miles, for an eight-year-old, gives a fella a lot of thinking time. Though this awful arrangement didn't make sense there would easily be plenty of bad stuff to report back to Grandpa. Unfortunate for me though, the longer spring day provided more than enough daylight for the chores Junior had saved. Quietly, with no one else in ear shot, I said, "If we are going to have this Shorty fellow come around this would be a good time to start, right now."

Planting Season

Rain fell hard every day for the two weeks after the funeral. Already April, we usually had our cotton seeds in the ground by mid-April. But this year Daddy had been sick the entire spring. We didn't get any farming done as a consequence. Mama put in her tomatoes, turnips for collard greens, black-eyed peas with a few rows of snap beans, okra, cucumbers and a small patch of watermelons. With Sara's help Mama would tend the vegetable garden while Junior and I worked with Daddy planting the cotton.

Wes wasn't big enough to help out a lot. Daddy had him bring us water or anything not too heavy for him to carry. Mama sent Wes out with our lunch, something like last night's dinner, leftover beans, with warmed up cornbread. Our little brother complained about the weight of the basket or how far he had to go up the hill from the house to the field. Little kids always find something to complain about. When the urge hit me to say something to him about being a big baby, Daddy reminded me who Wes' boss was, admonishing me to leave him alone. Meanwhile, my work all day long consisted of carrying heavier things like bags of seed or picking up big rocks the plow exposed.

Daddy did the plowing, but last year, at age ten, Junior started to learn so he could give Daddy a break once in a while. Our mule, Jane, had no problem whatsoever pulling the plow through the hard-packed dirt except for her attitude. Daddy said even a dumb animal like a mule can have an attitude. The one Jane had could be downright unruly at times. If you turned your back on her too long while working on the harness for the plow she would look around taking a mean bite from the middle of your back. We didn't wear shirts most days, owing to the oppressive summer heat. Having a mule with an attitude bite you on the back could ruin the best of days. She wasn't too bad about kicking unless a dog chased her or nipped at her from behind. Daddy said she would bite us because she didn't respect us enough. He said she thought she was in control, not us.

Daddy must have been right because she never hinted at biting him. He told us a mule takes control by getting another mule to move their feet. Sometimes, when grooming her or putting her in the barn for the night, Jane would try to step on my feet. Daddy said causing me to move my feet convinced her she had control. Horses and Mules get each other to move as a strategy for reaching better grass to feed on or to get a better spot at the drinking hole. Heck, lots of days in the spring we never wore any shoes. A big mule stepping on my foot with shoes on would be bad enough but without any on was unthinkable. She could have all the control she wanted.

Once, when we first got Jane, Uncle Wesley had been helping Daddy put her up for the night. Uncle Wesley, as noted earlier, used pretty bad words sometimes. If those same words came out of my mouth around Daddy, Mama or especially Sara the back-end of my overalls would get burned up by somebody's hand or a big switch. Well, this time Jane must have wanted to control my uncle. She stepped over on top of his foot as if aiming to nail it to the ground. Putting her fifteen-hundred pounds of weight down, she stood unmoving, as if his foot offered the one place in the barn for a mule to stand. My brother and I learned more words in the next couple of minutes than we ever got comfortable using in front of grown-ups or any time.

Uncle Wesley did everything possible to get her to move but she evidently wanted complete control. Beating her on the side with his fist while yelling a bunch of those bad words didn't make Jane blink an eye. Evidently, our mule didn't know those words meant for her to move. She didn't think about moving until Daddy came around giving a simple, gentle push of her nose to make the mule move straight back. Taking one step she moved off my uncle's foot. A gentle push on her nose is all it took. Uncle Wesley having his foot stomped offered a better lesson for Junior and me about being in control of a mule than getting bit in the back ever could. We were laughing so hard Uncle Wesley would have killed us both, but barely able to hobble around for the next hour there was little chance of him catching us. As our uncle continued to spew out those new words the look on Junior's face indicated he hadn't heard them either. Apparently, Jane didn't have enough respect for Uncle Wesley. He for sure didn't have control over her.

But this year we didn't have Daddy to help with Jane or the plowing. After the rain stopped for a few days Mama said we needed to get in the fields to get the cotton crop planted. The price of cotton had gone from thirty-cents per pound right after the Depression started all the way down to six cents by 1933. We got about fifteen bales out of our acres. At thirty-cents per pound fifteen bales brought in $2400 for our crop before but now we were lucky to get $500. Mama said we were fortunate though because tenant farmers and sharecroppers rarely made enough each year to pay what they owed their landlord for supplies.

Another stroke of good fortune, in her mind, was Grandpa Cook giving Daddy the farm in the first place. An awful lot of work went into making the measly $500, the total amount of money we had for Mama to buy the things we couldn't grow like cloth for clothes, kerosene for our lamps, medicine, and the doctor bills for Daddy being sick such a long time.

She woke us before daylight the first Tuesday to begin working the fields. The elation over finding out we didn't have to go to school became short lived once we found out why.

While we sat half asleep eating our biscuits with sorghum molasses she said to Junior, "Shorty, the man who is going to help you boys, is out at the barn putting the harness on Jane. Ya'll finish up your food and show him which fields to start on."

Her announcement caused me to stop eating altogether. Having neither seen nor heard any more about the black stranger since my talk with Grandpa Eddie, I hoped the plan for him to come around our farm had been changed.

Begging a last-ditch protest I said, "Mama, we don't need help from anybody. Junior and I can get the plowing done by ourselves."

She faced the wood stove continuing to take more biscuits from the oven. Junior gave me one of those looks indicating my comment was stupid, to shut up and eat my breakfast.

After a short silence Mama, with her back still turned, said, "John Thomas."

When she used my real first name including my middle name the situation had gone sour. She didn't in any way shape or form answer my question saying, "John Thomas, I want you to ask Shorty what you can do to help today."

Facing Junior she added, "And I want you to tell me tonight how well Johnny did everything Shorty tells him to do."

All the instructions were given in her usual calm, quiet voice. Though she gave the orders in a non-threatening way, without any doubt, if things didn't go well the potential outcome wasn't pleasant to think on.

Junior responded with a simple, "Yes Ma'am," while smothering two more fresh hot biscuits with molasses. Sitting speechless, anything said could result in pain for me, either physical or mental. Sara sat silent across from me with her closed-lip smile, the one signaling her being thrilled to death with the direction the breakfast talk had taken. Things weren't going well though the day had barely begun. Wes still lying in his warm bed didn't seem fair either.

Figuring Junior wouldn't see or hear everything all day long provided at least one positive outcome for the morning. Any problem with our new found helper would have to occur in private between him and me. Mama would certainly believe me over the black man.

Meanwhile, Junior finished his breakfast, jumped up from the table and said, "Come on Johnny, we gotta get going."

"But I'm not done yet."

"You should have spent more time eating and less time talking this morning," Mama put in, "Now go help your brother and Shorty, get going and don't forget what I said."

The stranger had caused me trouble already though he hadn't been seen by me since the cemetery. Reluctant to miss the rest of my breakfast I took my time scooting my chair back while grabbing a biscuit to take along.

"I won't forget," were my muffled parting words shoving a biscuit in my mouth while heading for the back door.

Going through the door something reminded me again about Wes still sleeping. He never had to get up as early as Junior and me. None of this had the slightest hint of fairness. Grandpa Eddie always told us life wasn't fair which didn't make me feel any better. My brother got to sleep while the rest of us couldn't. Grandpa always being right about things baffled me. The short trip from our back door to the barn gave me time to think about plenty of important matters.

Our barn looked more like a large outbuilding than a real barn. Grandpa Lewis had a real barn. Farming those thousands of acres required an enormous barn though the main use was for his horses. A majority of the horses Grandpa raised were sold to the Memphis Police Department. The fields, paddocks and exercise pens were filled with twenty or more geldings, mares, and foals. Grandpa kept no more than one or two studs at any one time. According to him, studs were too difficult to deal with. He believed more than one wasn't necessary anyhow. One stallion could produce a lot of babies every year. Grandpa Lewis could have written a book about horses. He probably had more knowledge of horses than anybody else in Mississippi. Once the buyer for the police department said one of the horses looked too fat.

Grandpa said, "A fat horse is a healthy horse."

The buyer not only believed him and bought the horse, Grandpa convinced him to pay extra. Anyhow, our barn wasn't big enough for more than one mule. We had a stall for Jane with enough space for our two cows to come in during bad weather. There was also room for storing hay as well as the few tools we needed, but little else. Out our back door, we had a backyard of sorts, mostly for the chickens to run around in. The barn, sitting thirty yards from the house, far enough to keep barn odors away, had been built long before any of us kids were born. Nowhere in sight, Junior had already gone inside the barn. Two wide doors on the front swung open to allow large farm implements to go in though we didn't have anything bigger than our mule. One remained closed with the other swung open allowing light from a kerosene lantern to shine through the opening onto the ground in front of the doors.

The sun had not come up yet but if we timed everything right dawn would be creeping up on us as we walked into the field. Trudging along half-awake behind Daddy leading the mule with Junior in front of me on foggy mornings in the fall created a picture in my mind no amount of money could buy from me now. Shadows cast from movement inside the barn danced on the ground outside with the clanking of metal against metal on the harness escaping as well into the yard. Getting closer a voice began to escape out through the door. Junior wasn't talking to himself. Someone else was talking to him.

As I stopped in the opened doorway the black fellow Shorty looked over smiling at me saying, "Good mornin Mister Johnny. I believe it's gonna be a fine day for plowin."

I looked over at Junior, sitting on a barrel waiting on me to show up for work. He looked back but didn't say anything.

"Come on over here, I was jiss tellin' Mister Junior bout the first time I ever put a harness on a mule, how's you got to make em respect you."

My senses couldn't take it. After what had happened at breakfast, now this fella started out tryin to convince me he knew as much as my daddy about mules. My reaction, like too many times in those years, caused my mouth to take over for my brain.

I shouted, "You don't know nothin about mules like my daddy did. And you can't talk like you do here in his barn."

Overwhelmed with confusion and sadness my feelings brought me to tears which I for sure didn't want either of them to see. Turning as quick as possible, running from the barn got me outside in front of the pig pen where I stopped. The crying was uncontrollable standing there in the dark all alone knowing Daddy couldn't help me. It seemed nobody else cared. After a minute or more the same voice came again from the open barn doorway.

Turning to look, Shorty stood there, a silhouette form with the light at his back, "Your brother says you knows how to put this harness on Miss Jane. I shur wish you would show me how you do it."

Difficult for me to believe, his request indicated maybe he didn't have a clue how the harness worked. Maybe he had been trying to impress us earlier. Or could it be he needed my help? Straightening myself, a quick decision was called for. This could present me with a chance to teach him a thing or two. Something may come out of it to report back to Grandpa Eddie, too. Walking back inside with him still standing in the doorway, my eyes met Junior who looked at me shaking his head.

"What?" I asked, angry for his lack of supporting me about the intruder.

"Nothing Johnny, just get the harness on Jane so we can get some work done before it's lunchtime."

Junior knew of my experience with the harness, limited to no more than a time or two which never included putting it on the mule by myself. Shorty came back into the barn standing off to the side with thumbs under the straps of his overalls saying nothing. Getting the harness on went well except for placing the collar over Jane's head. Every time I tried she raised her head just high enough an eight-year-old couldn't reach standing on tiptoes. Continuing to try several times began to get me quite frustrated.

Without hesitation, Shorty walked over laying a hand on her flank saying, "Whoa now Miss Jane."

Her eyes rolled back with ears forward as if listening hard, but otherwise she stood as quiet as Mrs. Shelby wanted us at reading time.

"She's ready Mister Johnny."

This time she kept her head still. With the broad, black, hand lying against her flank, she continued standing still, allowing me to complete the task. Within minutes, Shorty led her out into the yard, ready for work. Daylight grew stronger to the east by the minute working its way over the trees. The sky looked all shades of charcoal, pink and turquoise. Junior leaned over lowering the wick on the kerosene lamp into its channel to put out the flame. Starting toward the door, he gave me another look shaking his head back and forth like before.

"What?" I said, following him out the door. My brother never answered.

The acreage we planted lay in a flat spot on top of a hill beyond a stand of black walnut trees no more than two hundred yards from the house. With me standing off to the side, Junior told Shorty all about Daddy's approach to getting the crop planted.

'This is gonna be interesting,' I thought, convinced this guy would be more trouble than anything else.

Shorty said, "Well, I'm sure yer daddy knew the best way to get this job done. That's jiss how we'll do it."

I thought, 'Of course Daddy knew the best way. This fellow would probably take twice as long as Daddy planting our cotton in all kinds of crooked rows.'

Junior told him how he would take a turn once in a while giving Daddy a break.

Shorty replied, "That's fine by me. We'll do this job jiss how you wants to." Looking back he said to me, "Ain't that right Mister Johnny?"

Agreeing with him on anything would take an act of Congress or Sheriff Barton coming around threatening to throw me in jail, or both. Of course Daddy did it the right way. Caught in a trap, how could I say no while not wanting to say yes? Instead of answering him outright I chose to direct my response to Junior instead saying, “My brother knows how to do it. Daddy taught him.”

Nothing more was said on the matter. Shorty began talking to Jane as if she could understand his broken English or like she had known him forever, or both. Without a hint of reluctance, she set out at a slow walk. They stopped twice before lunch so the stranger and the mule could get a drink of water but otherwise worked through the entire morning. He never asked Junior to take a turn not stopping again until dark, moving at the same steady pace all day long. Amazingly, Jane kept going in a straight line for him. Each time they passed by he would be singing some ancient gospel song to himself or saying something in a quiet tone to the mule.

Later at dinner, Mama asked how our day went.

Junior said, “Shorty never stopped all day long except for water or a little while for lunch. He got more done in one day by himself than Daddy and I could while working together.”

“That’s not true. He didn’t get more done than Daddy could.” To me saying anyone did anything better than Daddy insulted him as well as our family.

Junior barked back, "You know it's true. I suppose you would say Shorty didn't help you get the harness on Jane this morning?"

"Well, he didn't. I got her harness on by myself with him standing there doing nothing but watching."

My story wasn't a total untruth, at least to me, though it required a little stretching. Junior had learned long before arguing with me would be a waste of time. He had begun a habit of having me stew over things rather than give me the satisfaction of fighting over them. Once he made his point on something, listening to my side wasted his time and his breath having to go back and forth. My big brother would be right more times than not though it never stopped me from an argument.

Addressing me no further, Junior looked up at Mama saying, "Shorty is gonna be a big help around here. I'm glad Grandpa Eddie got him to come around." Nothing I could say would make any difference. My brother had said the unthinkable. Throwing my fork onto my plate of beans while shoving my chair back, I ran out the back door all the way down to the lake. Junior's report had caused me to leave half my dinner after never getting to finish my breakfast at the beginning of the day. Now the stranger had caused me to go hungry.

Getting the cotton planted with enough time to grow before cold weather in the fall had Junior worried. Starting no later than mid-March we always got finished before the end of April.

Walking to the fields the second day Junior asked Shorty, “Daddy always said we had to get the cotton planted before the first of May. Starting this late, I don’t see how we can get finished. Do you think we should plant all fifty acres?”

Never slowing his pace or looking back, Shorty led Jane along the path up the hill saying, “Well we’ll jiss have to see. We’ll do the best we can. If’n the weather don’t mess with us, we might jiss plant all them acres.”

“But how can we get all those acres done by then?”

Again without looking back, Shorty’s short response was, “We’ll see Mister Junior, we’ll see.”

We did see too. Every day Shorty and Jane plowed more than the day before. Junior plowed once in a while just for practice. Jane worked pretty good for Junior but close to quitting time in the evening she would sometimes decide to quit before Shorty said we were done. Her stubbornness showed up any number of ways like stopping at the end of a field, closest to the way home, standing there facing the way she knew would take her to the barn. No amount of mouth noises or slapping the reins on her backside made her pick up one hoof.

My brother pulled as hard as he could on the bit to make her mouth plenty uncomfortable, but with no real effect. The saying, 'Stubborn as a mule,' must have come from someone who knew Jane. But when she saw Shorty coming over to help she would raise her head, throw her long ears back, and make the turn for Junior heading down the next row. She sensed the big fellow wouldn't take no for an answer. The sight of a switch in his hand scared her more than the whacking on the back of her hind legs.

Junior couldn't get close enough to use a switch while holding the plow up at the same time. She must have known because she didn't care even if he had a big stick in his hand. It became apparent right away Shorty had worked on somebody's farm in his earlier years. Someplace along the way, he learned an awful lot about how to handle mules.

Those few days when we had a full moon with clear skies, we kept plowing until long after dark. I've never been as tired at any other time in my life. We finished planting all fifty acres on the 28th of April. Somehow we planted two acres per day which people didn't believe possible with one man working behind one mule. To my dismay the first month went by without me finding anything bad about Shorty to report to Grandpa Eddie. There must have been things slipping by me each day or else maybe he kept me too busy to notice. Late in the evenings there wasn't enough energy left in me to spend thinking on the problem.

Plowin' Behind the Barn

Once we finished planting and the cotton began coming up the chopping started. Thinning out the new plants, mounding up the good ones, while keeping the weeds from growing, required plenty of chopping. This work could only be accomplished with a hoe bent over digging into the dirt all day long. We chopped throughout the summer, but this wasn't as time intensive as the planting leaving us time for other activities, the best of which was not work. Summer had always been the worst time for sleeping. The wood stove made our kitchen the hottest part of the house. Virtually no air moved inside except a whisper coming through the screen doors in the evenings. Getting up early became a better option than rolling around on top of clammy, sweat-soaked sheets trying to go back to sleep. Though sleeping with air-conditioning these years afterward I've woken up earlier than most people the rest of my life which, no doubt, is a result of those hot nights long ago in Mississippi.

The summer I was eight, my older brother and I spent time at Grandpa Lewis's around the horses whenever we could. The chores he always had for us were welcomed as they provided the perfect excuse for staying longer. Once in a while, Grandpa allowed us to ride two horses out across his farm. Though indicating they needed exercise, I'm pretty sure he used it as an excuse to justify his grandsons fooling around with them. He insisted we cool them down, giving them a good brushing afterward which seemed a small price to pay. We felt like cowboys riding across the old west. As long as we didn't ride through any freshly planted fields, Grandpa didn't care where we went. Riding out in the wide open alongside my big brother or trotting down a path alongside a cotton field next to a wooded area was the best of times. Sometimes we saw a covey of quail running on the ground ahead of us just before they took flight fifteen different directions into the trees.

Having different horses each time we rode gave us an excuse to test how fast they were, so we raced. Junior rode well but once in a while got the slower horse. Being the little brother, beating him had a special meaning to me, though it happened on a rare occasion. Why winning against him held such significance is beyond me.

Our family went to Grandpa Eddie's almost every Sunday after church to have lunch. Being at their place had a different feel altogether than Grandpa Lewis'. A great cook, Grandma Mattie served us fried chicken. The best part of those

Sunday visits, to me, was being asked by her to kill a couple of chickens for lunch. She cooked two when our big family came around. Grandma let Junior and me have the task. Though a gruesome job, we got the hang of it long before with our own chickens. We would bet each other as to how far each chicken could run after we chopped off its head. Picking the feathers off the dead birds was the worst part, not hard, just boring. Gutting a chicken, to me, was little different from gutting a big rabbit. Following her out the back door Grandma Mattie, Junior and I would all three stop while she decided who the victims would be. Grandma had names for all her animals including the chickens of which there were at least twenty or more around at all times.

"Boys, take Millie there," she said pointing one Sunday to a hen scratching in the dirt close to her petunias. "She's quit laying which means her time is up. And let's find out how tough old Tom is too. He's been fightin with that young banty rooster Freddie more and more lately. I'm afraid he's gonna kill Freddie one day. I need Freddie around to keep these hens bringing more chicks along. All Tom is good for is fightin and wakin up half the county every morning. Be careful though; he's got some pretty good spurs on him. He's a big un too."

With those instructions, she turned to head back in the house not waiting for any questions or confirmation. We knew what to do. Catching Millie became our first order of business. All we had to do was throw some fresh corn on the ground. She, with most of the others, would come running. The corn feed distracted her enough for me to walk up behind, bend over quickly and grab her. Hens like Millie never gave much of a fight when caught except a lot of cackling, chicken verbal complaining but after a few seconds, they would get quiet not knowing how it would end.

Roosters, on the other hand, were usually harder to catch. Some of them got quiet like the hens when caught but some were fighters. We figured Tom would be a fighter. Known not only for fighting with the other roosters, Tom could hold his own fighting a dog or a large cat. We planned to corner him next to the shed. Junior would grab him. Grandma made a good observation about the size of the spurs on the back of his legs. Neither of us wanted those cutting tools gouging away at our hand, arms or face. Maybe Tom heard Grandma say he would go into the frying pan alongside Millie. He was no place to be found after we caught her giving her the quick chop of the ax.

We spent the next thirty minutes corralling him. Junior grabbed him up against the side of the shed next to some old empty cans.

After a lot of wing flapping including more cackling than Millie, he surprised us by being more docile. Junior had to hold him at arms-length at first to keep from being pummeled. To our dismay, neither chicken did much running with their heads lying chopped off on the cutting block. After a few steps they each fell over flopping around a bit. So I won both bets since Junior said they would run around for at least a count of five.

Grandma Mattie made the best fried chicken. Millie had tender meat on her but old Tom's breast meat was like biting into a thick pork chop, though tasty. On occasion, Grandma had sweet tea. With sugar in short supply, which made it expensive, my grandparents had Grandpa's salary from the railroad which helped them get by better than a lot of folks. Our Daniels grandparents had fewer things to entertain us at their place with the food and chicken killing being the highlights.

Grandpa Eddie always invited Shorty for those Sunday meals. The Sunday Grandma had fried up Millie and the rooster Tom, Junior and I sat on the front porch with Grandpa and Shorty. Grandpa sat in his rocker smoking one of his favorite pipes. My brother and I were revisiting the beheading of the oversized rooster. Shorty sat whittling something he said would be a horse once he finished but looked more like a short-legged hippo with a horsetail. Grandma came out to announce lunch was ready.

She usually sent Sara but this time stuck her head out the screen door saying, “Lunch is ready. You boys come on in to get washed up. Shorty, you come in too, I set a place for you at the table and would be happy for you to join us.”

He said politely, “No, thank you anyways Miss Mattie. Black folks ain’t supposed to eat with white folks. That’s the way it’s always been. I’ll jiss have my dinner out to yer kitchen if it’s all right with you folks.”

Grandma wanted to insist at first, but Grandpa stopped her saying, “That’s okay, we want Shorty to eat where he is comfortable. If he wants to eat in the kitchen, it’s fine by me.”

As the rest of us followed into the house, Grandma led Shorty to the kitchen shaking her head the entire way. While not getting a vote or a say of any kind, having dinner sitting next to a black fellow seemed to me as though we would be taking things a bit too far. Sitting at the table with a plate full of old Tom and mashed potatoes waiting on Grandpa to say the blessing, I pondered their conversation though couldn’t understand why they needed to have such a discussion. Why didn’t we leave things as they were? Shorty’s decision to eat in the kitchen made me happy. Besides, what could we talk about sitting at the table with a black man? At home, Mama would fix breakfast for Shorty before we ever got out of bed. He took his other meals on our back porch or in the barn if we had terrible weather. To me, if we had to have him around at all, it made sense for him to eat on the porch.

Fortunately, Grandpa Eddie never once asked me to report on the unsavory findings from my daily interactions with the fellow. We had such a busy summer I missed Shorty's miscues though there must have been some.

Though admittedly nothing bad, something significant came to light later in the middle of the summer. One July day after chopping cotton all afternoon I began feeling sad, missing Daddy. Having sat by myself in the barn, Shorty came over sensing something bothered me. Junior had gone inside to clean up for dinner. Shorty made a point of keeping his distance from me. Though never saying anything to his face, my distaste for him must have been obvious.

But this time he came over anyhow saying, "Mister Johnny, what's troublin you?"

Hesitating at first, somehow it seemed okay to tell him. "I'm just a little sad."

"What's makin you sad boy? Is you sad bout yer pappy?"

Crying in front of grownups was avoided whenever possible, especially in front of him. To an eight-year-old farm boy crying showed a sign of weakness acceptable for girls or grown women but not men, except at a funeral of course.

Looking out the barn door it took all the courage I could muster. My answer was a simple, "Yeah, yeah I get sad some days thinking about him. I miss him a lot."

And so far I wasn't crying.

He sat next to me. Looking straight ahead he spoke softly saying, "I know what you mean. My pappy died a long, long time ago when I was jiss ten years ole and I still get sad."

It was the second time he mentioned his daddy dying. Thinking over what he said took me a minute or so though the kindness in his voice made me feel better right away. In his early fifties, he struck me as an ancient walking relic. The idea of him being sad for somebody who died so long ago gave me something to ponder.

Turning to look him in the face I asked, "Really, you mean you still miss your daddy after all those years?"

"I sho does. My pappy was the kindest, most nicest man I ever knowed til I met yer grandpa, Mister Eddie."

Not knowing what to ask about next, as usual, my mouth took control, "Did your daddy have a cancer?"

"No, no he didn't have no cancer." From his short non-answer, even an eight-year-old could tell the man didn't want to say anything more which didn't stop me from asking.

"If it wasn't a cancer what did he die from? Did he have some kind of accident?"

Looking hard into his face for the answer, as his lips had not yet begun to move, I waited. Sitting quietly for a little, a tear began to trickle down his face, the first time he ever cried in front of me. Well, it wasn't a lot of crying, one tear ran down his cheek which got wiped off in a hurry from a swipe of a big brown opened palm.

He turned looking at me straight on saying, "He didn't have no accident, he was kilt. He got kilt by a bunch of white men. That's alls I can say bout it right now. It still gets me angry all these years later."

'Damn,' I said to myself, careful to never say damn out loud.

White men killed his daddy. I'm white as is my whole family. But him having said something about Grandpa Eddie being nice gave me hope he didn't hate us.

"But never you mind bout that right now. It's okay for you bein sad sometimes bout yer daddy. If you ever wants to talk about it with me I'd be glad to."

"Shorty, do you think someday you can tell me what happened to your daddy?"

His face became one big smile, as big as a person can make without opening their lips. "I suppose I can when you gets a might older. It's a pretty hard story to hear even if you ain't a black man. Right now why don't we go get ourselves some of yer Mama's cornbread."

"Okay, but why did you say the part about my Grandpa Eddie being nice?"

"Oh, that's easy, yer grandpa treats all peoples the same. It don't matter to him what color they are or if they have any money or a shirt on their back. He don't care if they are big or small, fat or skinny, smart or dumb. He looks at every mans the same and treats me better than any white mans I ever knowed."

Everything Shorty said gave me a lot to consider. Suggesting white people might not mind the story of his daddy's death was troublesome. In my mind, hearing about another person getting murdered should be hard for anybody regardless of the listener's color, the murdered person's color, or even the story teller's color.

Without question, he had it right about Grandpa Eddie. He seemed to know my grandpa as good as I did.

I said, "So, what do you think makes people decide they are going to treat someone bad?"

This time he sat up straight. "Oh my honey, you done asked a big question now. I spect that's one of the biggest, mos hardest questions in the worl."

Another non-answer, answer, but feeling good about having asked such a hard question incented me to continue, “Well, what do you think?”

“Let me see if’n I can explain it this way. To my way of thinkin peoples don’t jiss decide they is gonna be mean to others, they learn it. Folks learn when they’s chillren not to like others cause they parents teached em. They folks taught em not to like peoples jiss cause they’s different in the way they act or else maybe they’s got a different color skin. That can make peoples mean toward others.”

“Why would people teach their kids to be mean?”

“Well, they don’t exactly sit down tellin em to, least not always. No sir, they don’t have to. The chillren learn easy enough hearin what their folks say and watchin what they do. You ever seen how baby ducks follow they mammy into the water when you come walkin by? She headed for the water for safety without sayin a thing with them babies learnin to follow. Once they gets older when they mammy is gone they jiss get in the water when they need to be safe. They might not know why they is doin it. It’s the same with peoples. If the chillren hear they pappy and mammy say bad things about folks who’s different they gonna grow up doin the same thing, not all the time but mos likely they gonna. It’s a hard thing to unlearn what you done learnt.”

It sounded simple and made plenty of sense.

"I guess so," I said.

With me wondering how somebody could be mean enough to kill his daddy we walked side by side in silence. But, the conversation gave me a bit of anxiety as to whether Shorty liked me or not. How could he possibly like me with my indications of disliking black people? Though the issue of him being around our place all the time wasn't resolved in my mind, I wanted him to like me at least a little for probably the first time. Also, being nice to me confused me too, since I for sure wasn't nice to him.

As we reached the screen door I stopped saying, "Can I ask one more question?"

"You sho can; you can ask all the questions you want. We's jiss gonna get hungrier with all these questions."

"It's only one more thing."

With a serious look on his face, he knelt beside me asking, "What's botherin you?"

"Well, would you mind not calling me honey?"

He pulled his head back slightly and squinted, not answering right away.

I added, "Well, it makes me feel like a girl."

He began scratching the side of his head. Smiling he said, "I says honey cause I cares bout you but I can see you look at it different from me. I agrees with you though. I'm fine with plowin them fields behind the barn first."

"What, what do you mean, plowin behind the barn?"

"I spect we better talk about plowin another time, you go on in the house and tell your mama I'll take a plate to the barn."

During dinner, I asked Mama if I could talk to Shorty about something afterward.

Junior interrupted, "What are you botherin Shorty about?"

Mama said, "Junior, you don't need to stick your nose into their business."

Looking back to me she added, "If it's okay with Shorty, but make sure you don't stay too long. You know we have another long day of work tomorrow." Her response surprised me at the time but makes sense now. She must have liked the idea of me spending time with him. If anyone could change my mind about Shorty it would be Shorty.

"I don't think he'll mind Mama. I'll take him some extra biscuits and ask him when I'm done. I'll make sure to get back soon enough."

He had just walked out of the barn when I came out the back door, the sun had gone down. The sky had become reddish purple prompting me to grab a kerosene lantern with a few matches. He said he would take the biscuits to his place for later. Planning to walk down the hill close to the road we would be away, out of listening range for Sara or Junior, especially Wes. If you wanted anything told to everybody all you had to do was tell Wes. My conversation with Shorty wasn't secretive in any way, but I wanted the discussion to remain private. Unbeknownst to me, the relationship had begun to improve ever so slightly.

As we approached the main road, I began my new line of questioning, "What did you mean about plowin behind the barn?"

"I wondered if you was thinkin on our last conversation. Well, you see, we was talkin bout peoples bein mean to others jiss cause they don't like the way other folks might be different from themselves. I got to thinkin that talkin or lookin different ain't the onliest reasons. You see, peoples sometimes jiss thinks about things different from the next fella. If'n they end up fightin peoples can get to where they don't like each other one bit."

The look on my face told him he had lost me.

"Okay, look, here's where plowin come in. What if you think plowin that small field behind the barn first is the best way, but your brother Junior wants to plow them up the hill. What are you gonna do cause the two of you is thinkin about it different but neither one is wrong or bad, they's jiss different? If you can't agree on what to do is there any chance you might fight over it? Now, before you answer, I knows they's a good chance you would. I done seen you fight over near bout anything more than once."

"Okay, but what if my way is the best?" I asked.

He didn't hesitate before starting again, "Who gets to decide which way is best. I done said neither way was wrong or bad."

"Yeah, but even if my way is best doesn't mean I think his way is wrong or bad."

"You makin my point for me. You both is probably thinkin yer way is best but that ain't the point. The point is you both is lookin at the situation different. You both got yer own reasons too. Ifn you was to fight and win you could plow behind the barn first, but alls you done is hurt your onliest big brother makin him do something he don't want to."

"You mean if my brother wants to go down to rob Watson's store I shouldn't try to talk him out of it if he thinks it's okay but I don't?"

"No sir I ain't sayin nothin of the kind. They's man's laws and they's God's laws. We all gots to try our best to obey all them laws, whether we agree with em or not. No, I'm talkin bout most of the other things that come along in life there ain't no clear right or wrong bout. Sometimes peoples jiss wants somethin different than somebody else like plowin behind the barn or up on the hill. You got to learn how to accept most ways folks is different, so you don't end up fightin with em or not likin em anymore."

"You mean I should always give in to my brother?"

"Nope, don't meant that neither. You ain't the onliest person havin to give in, we alls got to learn to give in now once in a while. We got to quit goin round tryin to change everybody's mind jiss cause they lookin at things a different way. Peoples is always goin around tryin to make other peoples live they whole lives different. You gotta let peoples live like they want to if'n they don't do no harm to nobody. They got to get their way some time whether you think it's the best or not. Goin around tryin to change peoples all the time jiss cause their way is different is like stirrin up a hornets nest. Somebody always gonna get stung now. The more peoples end up fightin over they differences the more they gets to thinkin they don't like each other bein as they is jiss too different."

The conversation made me think about my grandpas. "I suppose you noticed my two grandpas don't like each other one bit."

With a quick response, shaking his head Shorty said, "Oh, now, they is truth in them words, but I ain't got no business gettin caught up in it."

"Oh, no, I don't mean for you to take sides or anything. I'm pretty sure you like Grandpa Eddie better anyhow because of how he treats you. But what I'm wondering is how two people can get angry enough at each other to stay mad for so many years."

We walked a little further, both of us quiet, before he answered, "Well, this whole time we been talkin bout folks treatin others bad on account of bein different or lookin different or thinkin different. I spect your two grandpas done jiss bout the same thing a long time back. I spect one of em wanted to plow behind the barn while the other one wanted to plow up the hill. They must've got in a big fight over the matter, now none of them fields been plowed since."

Shorty was right, whatever issue created the discord between my grandpas, they never discovered a way to work through or else they never tried. One day maybe Mama would tell me what happened between them. Asking either grandpa which fields they wanted to plow would get nothing but funny looks or a bunch of questions. I decided to never allow myself to get as angry with anybody over differences as they had. We said goodnight. Watching him move off down the road I stood amazed at how smart the man was but after a few seconds began to consider carefully which fields would be the best to plow deciding the one behind the barn must be the right answer.

The Harlow Boys

Like every summer during my childhood, those hot months of 1933 passed in a hurry. Sometime in August Grandpa Lewis decided Shorty could move into an old house on his property no more than a quarter of a mile from us putting him a lot closer to us than the cabin on Grandpa Eddie's place. I'm sure Grandpa Lewis and Grandpa Eddie didn't talk to each other on the issue though. One day Shorty borrowed Jane with our wagon to move his bed and few pieces of furniture to the closer place which wasn't any bigger, no more than a one-room shack with a small fireplace. An old wood stove sat in the corner used as a kitchen. Grandpa Lewis said a Chickasaw Indian fellow lived there long before his Papa William ever owned the land. There were remnants of a handful of graves away from the cabin in the back. Junior said they couldn't be Indians since they buried the dead under their houses. It must have been something Mrs. Shelby talked about one of those days I sat contemplating my after-school activities. The idea of having dead people under our house caused a few sleepless nights. It wasn't something to think about much but seemed to jump inside my head at night lying in bed. Junior said we shouldn't mention anything to Shorty though. None of it ever explained the graves behind his place.

The little cabin sat a ways off the road right down the hill behind our farm toward the lake. Shorty slept there by himself but otherwise spent his time at our place either working or eating. One day in early September, Junior and I went with Shorty into Holly Springs. Jane pulled the wagon. Mama needed a fifty-pound sack of flour which Jane could carry without the wagon but we also had to pick up a couple of heavy parts for an old hay baler we were rebuilding. Grandpa Eddie and Junior found the rusty implement at a farm sale. Grandpa Lewis said if we could get the baler working we could harvest his acres of hay to make some money. Shorty said he could do the needed repairs but would have to replace several missing pieces. By then, to my way of thinking, the man could do anything he put his mind to.

Getting to town took us an hour. Jane never got in a hurry except when she headed to the barn. The trip into town obviously went in the wrong direction for her liking. It wasn't worth fussing with her over. We saved the fussing for plowing or other work around the farm. The town wasn't large, two-thousand people or so, at the time. Memphis, the nearest big city was a huge, busy place. Any time anyone needed something the stores in our town didn't have they would go up to Tennessee sure to find most anything in Memphis. But, Holly Springs was big enough to make it plenty interesting.

Daddy said during the Civil War General Grant's Yankee troops were storing supplies there to help them win the Battle of Vicksburg. But the Rebels came in and burned everything they had stored. Why the Yankees came down here going to war with us in the first place over the issue of Negro slaves made little sense. Though the year was 1933, countless white people in northern Mississippi still said they believed blacks were better off when they were slaves. Those same people said the majority of black people remaining poor after all those years proved they couldn't take care of themselves which didn't make any sense because Shorty took care of himself pretty well plus our family to boot. Though the black people we knew were poor, there were plenty of poor whites too. Besides, no one ever told me black people agreed with the idea. Thinking about asking Shorty any question on slavery made me more than a little nervous causing me to simply leave the issue unsettled.

The town had a main street with a town square where the courthouse stood. There were trucks and cars parked all around the square. Shorty stopped the wagon at the curb outside of Watson's Grocery. Old man Watson owned the biggest Grocery Store in town. His grandpa opened the store. He was one of the first people to settle in Marshall County. Mama had a charge account with Mr. Watson for everything she bought during the year. She settled up with him every November with whatever cotton money we made. Junior and I went in through the front screen door. Even though the temperature stayed somewhat cooler inside out of the hot sun, with ceiling fans moving the air around, Shorty chose to stay on the wagon. He could have come in but would have had to use the back door. Black people were not allowed to come through the front where whites came in. The same rule applied in all the stores in town.

In those days, that's the way things were, giving me plenty to think about. The color of a person's skin determined which door they would be allowed to use or which water fountain they could drink from in Woolworths. But most of us kids weren't curious enough to question the practice. Not until years later did I realize some people live their entire lives never wondering how the way they treat others can be downright hurtful. Sadly, it has become obvious over the years how some are either too busy living their own lives or else don't care enough to think about others feelings.

There's also those who understand what's going on but do nothing about it, while others try to make things better. Then there are people who think nothing whatsoever needs to change. My Grandpa Eddie believed strongly in fairness. He thought everybody should use the same door and drink from the same fountain. Grandpa Lewis, on the other hand, had the opinion the system in place worked fine. He believed everybody accepted it, whites and blacks. For me, the elusive answers were unclear. Multiple people, who had influence on me, had multiple opinions on the subject causing me all too often to move on to something else.

We didn't need Shorty's help this particular day anyhow. Junior would carry the flour to the wagon leaving the few other things Mama needed for me. Old man Watson stood behind the counter finalizing a transaction with Mrs. Wheeler.

Noticing us come through the door Mr. Watson said, "Hey boys, come on in, I'll be with you fellas in a minute."

Mrs. Wheeler looked around greeting us as well saying, "Hello Junior, Johnny. How is your mama doing?" Nice enough to your face, Mama said Mrs. Wheeler talked about everybody in town behind their back. As old as Grandma Mattie or older, Mrs. Wheeler sat beside Grandma every Sunday in church. Grandma didn't particularly care for it. We tried to avoid talking to Mrs. Wheeler but if we had to we rarely told her the truth about anything. If she went around all day making up stuff anyhow Junior and I figured we may as well have some fun.

Once Junior told her Mama got bit by a water moccasin causing her arm to swell up bigger than her thigh. The next Sunday in church Mrs. Wheeler told Mama Junior had filled her in about the snake bite asking if Mama's arm was any better. Before answering, Mama looked over at Junior who, having heard the older lady's question, stared straight ahead to the front of the church shaking visibly, trying not to laugh.

Mama answered, "Well, I'm doin much better Edith, thank you for asking. The snake was just a baby."

Mrs. Wheeler either didn't care or wasn't smart enough to know a bite from a baby moccasin could be every bit as dangerous as one from a full-grown snake. Later Mama fussed at Junior for telling lies but gave him a wink more or less admitting she added the part about the baby snake. After the snake story we began to wonder how often Mama told Mrs. Wheeler the truth. Maybe nobody did. Maybe the old woman never made up anything about people. It's possible she did nothing more than repeat what everyone else told her never having anything true to tell.

This time Junior had a different tale for her. My guess is he came up with something right as he saw her after walking into the store.

"Mama's better Mrs. Wheeler, but she had an awful bad day last Monday."

"Oh, I'm sorry to hear that. Did something bad happen at the farm?"

"Well, yes ma'am sort of. You see, Mama took a bucket of slop out to the hogs, slipped and fell right in with the big hog we call George. Now, George, he jumped right on top of her in a heartbeat. That fat rascal could have hurt Mama somethin terrible if Johnny and I hadn't been right there."

The old woman stood with eyes wide, her mouth opened. Mr. Watson stood hidden by the cash register with a smirk on his face. "Well, did you boys help your mama, what happened?" She obviously couldn't wait to hear the rest. Junior had done an excellent job of storytelling drawing me in as well. I wanted to find out how it ended too.

"Oh we sure did, I yelled out to George. George is the hog's name. I yelled out, 'George you get off my mama and back away or I'll make bacon out of you right now.' You know, that old hog looked up at me with a scared look on his face, spun around slinging mud everywhere, heading right back inside his barrel under the shade."

Not waiting for a response or saying anything more Junior walked right past her to the back of the store where Mr. Watson kept the sacked flour. Somewhat stunned she didn't say anything more. Looking over at me she got nothing more than a shoulder shrug besides watching me follow my brother to the back of the store. We didn't have as much fun the rest of the week. We used up all the fun for the week right there in the store. Heck, we never named our hogs; we just raised them up, killed em and ate em. As we finished our shopping, Mr. Watson told us we should take better care of our mama besides making sure George the hog behaved himself. Everyone knew we were jerking her around except, of course, Mrs. Wheeler herself.

Walking out the front door we heard two voices immediately recognizable as trouble. Standing next to the wagon looking up at Shorty were Teddy and Sam Harlow. Uncle Wesley told us about those two, Teddy twenty, his younger brother Sam eighteen. Our uncle said they were nothing but trouble adding we should steer clear of them. Both unmarried, they still lived on their daddy's farm on the opposite side of town from us. Uncle Wesley said they had been arrested by Sheriff Barton lots of times. He said they had a reputation for rowdy drinking and gambling more than good people would. They never robbed anybody or broke into any stores; at least none anyone could prove. Otherwise, they would have been hauled off to prison long ago. Drunken fights broke out on a regular basis among the men they gambled with.

Once, a fellow from Memphis came to town. He, with some others, had been gambling with the Harlows. Later the same night he got stabbed in the stomach. The out-of-towner died before getting to a hospital. The District Attorney's office investigated but never proved who killed the man. The people we talked to figured the Harlow boys had some involvement, but Sheriff Barton couldn't get any of the other gamblers to tell anything. The man who died bled to death before the Sheriff arrived, so he had nothing to say either.

The Harlow boys hated Negroes. Although I didn't like Negroes, I didn't hate them. Understanding how you could hate somebody took a lot of thinking. After all the thinking, the concept just cluttered up my brain, unresolved the same as too many other people issues adults couldn't even explain or deal with. Also, though my grandpas didn't like each other one bit, they didn't hate each other, or at least I didn't think they did.

Teddy and Sam had come over to the wagon after noticing Shorty sitting up top on the driver's seat.

Seeing us come out of the store Teddy said, "Hey Cook boys is this your Negro?"

The comment, though directed at us, without a doubt was meant to make Shorty mad.

Teddy continued, "You know it's against the law to own slaves any more but this one here looks like a fine sturdy one. Now, you boys didn't buy this here Negro did you?"

They laughed at their own joke. At eleven-years-old my brother was smaller than either Harlow, but what he lacked in size he made up for with guts. Dropping the flour sack to the grocery store porch, Junior jumped off running over to Teddy Harlow attempting to give him a shove. The bigger, faster Teddy side stepped Junior pushing him to the pavement.

Shorty made a move to get off the wagon when a voice came from behind me. Mr. Watson yelled out, "Hey...Teddy, you and your brother get on away from here. Leave these boys alone. I'll call the Sheriff if I have to."

Junior got up from the pavement, both hands bloodied from breaking his fall on the concrete. Shorty eased back down onto the wagon seat.

Sam Harlow spoke, "We just wanted to find out how these Cook boys got them a Negro servant, that's all."

Mr. Watson wasn't having any of it, "I said you get away from here. I mean it, you get now."

Teddy looked up at Shorty, "We'll see you again, I can promise you that."

Shorty knew better than to touch either of those Harlow boys regardless of what they were doing. In 1933 a black man could be lynched for doing anything to a white man, not only in Mississippi, even if the white person started the trouble. Shorty said nothing. The look on his face said enough. With his eyes opened wide and head raised he leaned forward as if about to get up to take somebody's head off. Nothing could have been better than to see Teddy's head rolling out in the street.

After a short stare down between Teddy and Shorty, Sam said to his brother, "Let's go, Teddy, we got better things to do anyhow."

They didn't have better things to do; they probably had more trouble to get into someplace else.

As Mr. Watson went back inside the store, Shorty thanked him for helping us out. Junior climbed onto the wagon. Shorty placed a hand on his shoulder saying, "You is gonna make a fine man someday boy, a fine man. You gotta get some bigger, but I don't believe any man is gonna get away with doin you wrong."

But Shorty knew the threat from Teddy Harlow could be more than a mere warning. Later on, we learned Shorty had gone through his entire life working hard at being cautious around white people. He could never afford to offend even good white people with his comments or actions. Any misunderstanding around the good people could cause trouble for him with the bad ones. At the time none of us knew his history, but Shorty had experienced firsthand the kind of trouble brought on by people like the Harlow's. The episode in front of the grocery store got me thinking as we rode back to the farm. Something wasn't right. Those guys were trying to make Shorty mad but how could the Harlow boys be mean to him without knowing anything about him? Heck, I sure wasn't happy about having a Negro around our farm all the time, but so far he hadn't done anything to make me hate him. After our conversation about his daddy dying my feelings toward him had begun to change but couldn't mean I was starting to like him. No, it must have meant something else entirely.

Squirrel Dog

There wasn't much to look forward to about working in the cotton fields except, of course, getting out of school during harvest. My plan would have been to stretch out the time off, but Mama made sure we were in school right until the day we started picking. We went back the day after hauling our crop to the gin. We couldn't drag our feet during the harvest either. One frost would kill part of the leaves on the plant, which was fine, but repeated freezing and thawing hurt the bolls. Also, once the bolls were ready to pick, the more they got rained on, the lower their quality which meant less money for us. So once we started picking we picked hard all day every day until we got every acre harvested.

Meanwhile, before the cotton got ready to pick, in between school and chores at home, we took every chance we could to go hunting. Mama made a good squirrel stew. Squirrels don't have enough meat to fry them. Rabbits were big enough to fry like chicken. We never ate Possum but black people liked them. Squirrel meat with some potatoes, carrots, and onions made for one heck of a stew. Junior and I were allowed to hunt by ourselves as soon as we were big enough to handle a shotgun safely. Daddy taught us how to handle the guns. This would be the first year for me to prove I had grown big enough. Mama said okay as long as my brother went along, Shorty too. Having become somewhat more comfortable with the idea of having him around, I didn't mind him going along besides the fact he had a squirrel dog.

He named the dog Pepper, a mixture of terrier and two or three other breeds, weighing less than fifteen pounds. Shorty said he found the puppy on a section of rail track his road crew had been working on. Just a few weeks old he picked Pepper for the puppy's name because of his predominately white fur with black spots all over his back and legs. His ears were white with black spots too. Coming to our place every day Pepper stayed close to Shorty following right behind all day long. The little dog no doubt contributed to Jane behaving well for Shorty. She always kept track of the terrier. Whenever Shorty had to scold her about anything Pepper would light into her nipping at the mule's hooves especially if she quit plowing for no good reason. The smart, quick little dog would nip and bark, dodging in and out enough to get her going without getting stepped on or kicked or causing her to bolt away. Jane tried more than once to stomp him into the ground but he would scoot out of the way to a safe place long before her brain told her foot what to do.

Shorty informed us Pepper had become the best squirrel dog ever with the emphasis on ever. Well, having seen a lot of things in my eight years never had I seen a dog do anything more than retrieve a dead squirrel. The idea of a dog hunting for a tree-dwelling animal as small as a squirrel left a lot to ponder.

Junior got the twelve-gauge off its rack on the wall in Mama's room. Daddy always wanted a gun close by. He gave me the old eight-gauge which stayed in the corner behind the kitchen door. Shells were kept in a box high on top of Mama's Hoosier cabinet too high for small kids like Wes to reach. Distinguishing the twelve from the eight-gauge had been an early lesson, an important one too. The bigger eight-gauge shells wouldn't fit in the twelve-gauge barrel, but you could get the twelves into the eight-gauge gun. By not fitting snug, those smaller twelve-gauge shells could get jammed or send the explosion out the breach instead of the barrel. If Daddy told us once he told us a hundred times to double check which shells we had. Hunting interested me which made learning about hunting stuff easy. Not learning meant not being allowed to participate. Junior put a dozen shells for his gun in his pocket giving me the same number for mine. Shorty had a shotgun back at his cabin but decided not to bring it. He wanted us to do the shooting. Two guns would be plenty of squirrel killing firepower.

Junior tried to find out more about Pepper before we went out asking, "Hey Shorty, I've seen pictures of bird dogs. I've also seen real live coonhounds and Walker hounds for running deer but never anything like a squirrel dog? Are you sure you're not pulling our legs? How does this squirrel dog find a squirrel anyhow? Does he point?"

We laughed at the idea of a pointing terrier.

Shorty made no reply asking a question of his own, "Well, how does you and Mister Johnny find a squirrel?"

"We just stand back a long way in the woods, watch for something to move high in the trees and try to sneak up on em."

"Pepper does bout the same thing except he's got a nose better than all three of us put together. If'n he don't see em up in the trees he'll smell where they been on the ground, but that's not the best part."

I had to know, "What's the best part then. He does point, huh?"

Shorty laughed, "You boys'll jiss have to see for yerselves what the best part is. It's a lot easier showin ya than tellin ya. Let's get goin before all the daylight is gone. Pepper can sho nuf find em in the dark but we can't see em to shoot nothin."

This squirrel hunting outing had become more of an adventure than a simple fall hunt. Still, if Shorty had told nothing more than a bunch of tall tales about Pepper, at least the terrier should be able to catch anything we shot if it wasn't dead after hitting the ground. Having a wounded squirrel come out of the tree and run for a hole to hide in happened sometimes.

On the way out the back door to the wooded acres which stood between our place and the lake one more silly question came to me, "Does Pepper go up a tree to fetch a squirrel out of its nest?"

Shorty laughed his short staccato "heh, heh, heh" before saying anything without turning around, "Now I suppose that would be some kind of squirrel dog Mister Johnny, but no siree, he ain't no climbin or pointin pooch, you'll see."

We set out late afternoon, around four o'clock. Squirrels are more active early in the morning and again late in the afternoon. Hunting with Daddy we would split up after getting into the woods, Junior one way with me following Daddy another so we could cover more ground.

But this time Shorty said we should stay together, at least at first, if we wanted to watch him, "Work this here fine squirrel dog of mine."

Owing to the frequent trips from our house into the woods, well-worn trails had been created over the years. The deer, going back and forth from the woods to Mama's vegetable garden fashioned the ones not made by us. They liked the sweet corn the most. Out past the barn, we veered south to go through more than an acre of switchgrass and bluestem. Stumbling into a covey of quail happened more often than not. We never had a bird dog, but Daddy and Junior, with me following behind, had pretty good luck flushing the covey. We knocked down one or maybe two when the covey flushed. Daddy had an eye for watching where the singles landed which afforded a few follow-up shots resulting in one or two more downed birds.

Having less meat on them than squirrels, Mama cooked the breasts in a frying pan, each one wrapped in a slice of bacon which made a recipe of quail gravy a fine restaurant couldn't beat. Those small birds got off the ground in a hurry. Though fun to shoot at they were hard to hit. Daddy could hit them one after the other. Junior killed his share once in a while too. After getting old enough to hunt with them, I shot when the birds came up with success as random as my aim.

If a covey flushed it didn't matter if by accident or if we were hunting they would startle the heck out of all of us. This particular day we weren't hunting quail, though we had to always stay on alert.

Beyond the open fields, we had another fifty acres, a large stand of hardwoods and pine. Those woods were like a sanctuary for my brother and me. As soon as I got old enough to walk we went there every day possible to spend time by ourselves, long before Daddy allowed us to go hunting. Once we could hunt together, we were in the woods all the time. Oak, black walnut, and hickory with basswood trees mixed in made up most of the hardwoods. Southern pines standing over thirty feet tall had grown here and there. Junior said they were the sentinels of the forest. Because they were the tallest they kept watch for the rest of the trees including the animals. In our magical place, those tall trees reached up to the clouds guarding us along with the rest of the woods.

The squirrels could be found just about any place but liked to stay close to the oak and hickory trees once the nuts became plentiful. Stopping about fifty yards from the outside edge of the woods we scanned the trees for movement. Pepper stopped too with ears pointed toward the woods, his head turning side to side. If any squirrel had been in the trees along the edge it went unnoticed. My brother and I did nothing more than watch the dog.

After a moment, Shorty began moving once more at a slower pace before looking at the terrier saying, "Pepper, squirrel Pepper, find a squirrel, go get em."

The worked up bundle of muscle, bark, and brains, took a long look at his master as if thinking for a while before taking off as fast as his short legs would carry him bounding through the tall grass. Each time he bounced up his head pivoted looking for the trees before falling back below the grass line. More than once he changed direction in mid-air before finally disappearing into the woods.

"Now let's us jiss wait right here a minute or two," Shorty said with an open palm.

Junior and I looked at each other, shotguns held at our sides, barrels pointed to the ground, still unloaded as we were taught. Wondering what might happen next didn't matter because this squirrel hunt, off to an unusual start, would apparently be full of surprises. Not long after we heard Pepper's small terrier bark, yap, yapping another hundred yards into the woods.

"He's got one treed boys. Let's go," Shorty began moving before finishing his sentence.

Junior had started, too, right on his heels. Carrying a shotgun almost as long as I was tall created a challenge for me to keep up.

The barking slowed from a constant yapping to an occasional single bark. We first spotted the dog standing at the base of a massive white oak tree over sixty-feet high, maybe a hundred years old. At its base the terrier looked up into the leaves, his body shaking from the excitement of the hunt. Hunting season opened each year in September. The leaves made spotting game a tough task, even tougher if the squirrel became aware someone stood below looking up. Pepper looked over to acknowledge our presence. He had stopped barking altogether as if to indicate he had successfully called us to come see what he found.

"Good dog Pepper, where is he boy?" Shorty asked.

Continuing to squirm with more yapping the terrier put his front paws up onto the back side of the tree. Looking over at his master, he appeared to wait for a command to climb up.

"That's a pretty smart dog Shorty. He sure looks like he's on point, sort of. Now, if there's one up there it'll stay on the other side away from us. Johnny, you ease on around to the other side to see if we can make him move." Junior decided to employ our usual technique.

"No, you jiss wait right here Mister Johnny. Pepper, shake a bush Pepper, shake a bush."

Shorty had a different strategy in mind. Once again looking over to my brother, who had already turned his head my way, we shared expressions of wonderment. We were about to witness an unbelievable exhibition by an untrained animal the likes of which either of us would ever see again. The squirrel dog looked over his shoulder and back at his master, thinking about what should be done to act on his command. Pushing back off the tree he went over to a young, small Basswood tree covered in Muscadine vines eight or ten feet away on the same side of the tree as the squirrel. Grabbing the vines around the base and holding on he shook with his whole body as if killing a forty pound rat. The black, ripe Muscadine grapes began flying off, rattling around, smacking into the early fallen leaves like giant pieces of hail. The resulting noisy commotion would have scared a bear let alone a squirrel. Once, twice, and again for no more than ten seconds, the small tree top shook, the terrier hanging on, shaking so hard all four paws literally came off the ground.

"There he is now, who's gonna shoot him," Shorty whispered.

We both had difficulty taking our eyes off the action on the ground to see what the squirrel dog had caused to happen in the thick tree canopy above. Based on Shorty's observation Junior and I looked up but at first, saw nothing. In another few seconds something moved. Thirty feet above a slight breeze unfelt by us on the ground lifted tufts of grey fur off the squirrel where the scared creature stopped again to hide, hugging close to the tree trunk, from whatever made the bush shake. My brother and I were stunned. Shorty's dog shook a bush on command right in front of our eyes making the squirrel move as the owner expected.

Junior had loaded the twelve-gauge when we stopped but we never loaded the eight-gauge until right before we wanted to shoot. Though safe enough until the hammers were pulled back the old gun wasn't trustworthy when cocked. Two separate hammers fired each of two barrels.

"You take him," Junior said in a whisper, which was all I needed to hear.

In no time two fat shells were shoved into the breach, one hammer cocked with the second barrel saved for insurance. As slow as possible, to remain unnoticed, it took me several seconds to raise the gun pointing at the unsuspecting animal which had found a spot sitting in the crotch of a limb, its back against the tree. Now, an eight-gauge shotgun packs an enormous punch for shooter and target alike. My first experience with it came after insisting on learning to shoot with the smaller shotgun. Junior told me the twelve-gauge was the smaller of the two which, making no logical sense, caused me to shake my head at such an absurd attempt to trick me.

Comparing the shells or the barrels never occurred to me. He told Daddy I had argued with him wanting to start with the eight-gauge. Daddy's attempts to get me to try the twelve first failed also as history had taught me the two of them might be in a conspiracy to get me to shoot the bigger gun. The eight kicked a lot worse than the twelve is all they kept saying. Daddy had Junior place a couple of rusted cans on the fence posts beyond the outhouse for my first target. The explosion knocked me to the ground. Expecting this would be the outcome, Daddy made sure the gun didn't have but one shell in the breach. They had predicted the recoil would cause me to lose my grip on the gun on my butt's way to the ground. My shoulder and jaw hurt, though not as bad as my pride while they stood over me belly laughing. "I told you to keep your jaw out of the way," Daddy said still laughing while helping me off the ground, "are you okay son?" He loved to have a good time with us but always wanted to make sure we were not hurt, much more than necessary to make a long lasting impression.

"You should try the twelve-gauge. It truly doesn't have near as much kick."

But before shooting anything different I asked, "How come if the twelve is bigger the eight kicks more?"

Junior said, "I tried to tell him, Daddy. Johnny, the gauge size measures the number of lead balls the same size as the barrel needed to make a pound of lead. The barrel for the eight is bigger because it takes no more than eight balls as wide as the barrel to make a pound of lead. The smaller diameter twelve-gauge barrel takes twelve. The smaller the barrel, the smaller the shell, the less powder, the smaller the explosion."

He showed me the two shells side by side. Having seen the shells for both guns plenty of times, comparing them never occurred to me. Still, the entire explanation was a head-scratcher.

I said, "Why didn't you say so in the first place?"

Junior added, "I tried to but you went off to get the shells for the bigger gun. I wasn't gonna chase you around if you were gonna be stubborn headed about it."

Daddy confirmed it, "Your brother's right. You want to try the twelve-gauge now?"

The problem with having a brother who plays tricks on you is you don't know when to trust him and when not to.

A slight breeze continued to blow against the fur, revealing Pepper's squirrel sitting motionless high above us. Taking aim as close as possible, the shot must be quick before the animal made a run for a hole or nest. We learned never to shoot them in their nest because they would stay there dead or dying but never falling to the ground. In addition to leaving good meat at the top of the tree, our respect for the animal would not allow us to kill for the sake of killing.

Pepper stood quiet surrounded by a bunch of new fallen Muscadines underneath the young tree looking up for any movement. Shorty and Junior looked up too. We had been taught to take a breath and hold it. The next part though, a slow squeeze of the trigger, made anticipating the result almost unbearable. After my initial episode with the bigger shotgun had not worked out to my liking, mastering it became imperative. In an instant, the booming explosion filling the woods could have been heard from our farm halfway to Jackson. A cloud of gunpowder mixed with falling leaves made seeing difficult high above us, but as the air cleared we could see the squirrel, still up there. But, my target now hung on by the claws on its front feet. My shot tore into the back legs rendering them useless.

"Dang it," I half whispered to prevent scaring any other nearby game though anything within two miles heard the big gun go off.

Daddy taught us to always make a clean, humane kill. Shooting again might ruin all the meat if the best parts weren't already messed up. Before the thought occurred to regret my bad shot or take another one, he let go. No sooner had he tumbled through the leaves to the ground than Pepper jumped him. Taking it by the head, to avoid being bitten, the terrier shook the squirrel more intensely than the small tree. My brother and I watched in disbelief.

The authentic squirrel dog confirmed himself as a retriever too, trotting over to Shorty to drop the dead animal at his feet. The rest of the afternoon, we killed five more, every one of which Pepper had treed. His well-earned reward for the hunt's successful end, a nice pile of squirrel guts. Farm dogs liked fresh organ meats better than anything. All the good meat went in Mama's stew with a bunch of vegetables and herbs. Squirrel stew with hot biscuits made for a supper as if we were eating like royalty. Those meals made us forget for a short while how hard the times were.

We hunted often with Shorty and his dog with great success except for one particular time, a cold day in early November. The leaves off the trees made spotting game easier. Seeing squirrels up high became less challenging. But since everything seems to have a down-side, the leaves lying all over the ground made quiet walking difficult. Of course, neither of those made any difference to Pepper one way or the other. This afternoon we planned to hunt separately. Junior took Pepper with him. Shorty stayed with me. We found a good place to sit on a ridge which dropped off a steep bank to the lake over a hundred yards below. We chose a spot high enough we could look straight across into the bare limbs of a stand of large oaks thirty feet or more above ground. An overcast sky threatened early darkness increasing the difficulty of spotting grey fur against the background of greyish cloud cover. But not long after we sat down Shorty saw movement.

Two fat squirrels chased each other through the treetops in front of us at eye level. We called two at once a double but few doubles ever ended up in the stew pot. A single shot at the first target would result in everything nearby either hiding or running like the wind. Both squirrels spotted us. Stopping at the same time, they lay flat against the top of a limb showing nothing more than a few tufts of grey fur. Sitting still on the ground gave me the chance to safely load my shotgun.

Turning my head painstakingly I looked at Shorty from the corner of my eye whispering, “I’m gonna see if I can ease over to my right against a tree to get a clear shot.”

“Okay, jiss make sure you move slow as an ole snail as you look up in there but you gotta watch yer step at the same time. You best be careful now boy.”

Nodding my agreement before taking a lifetime to stand, I stopped perfectly still before taking any steps. Both squirrels lay unmoving, barely visible continuing to hug the limb. Their instincts told them they were either in a good spot or else they had waited too long to find one. The leaves underfoot were wet which helped me step quietly. One foot after the other, stopping along the way, moving ten feet to my cover tree took at least as long as building the Great Pyramids, or so it seemed. Finally, leaning hard against the trunk, I picked my first target leaving the other for a probable running shot. Cocking both hammers at once, one of few times to do so, my intention to save precious seconds for the next shot resulted in near disaster.

Holding the gun tight against my shoulder while taking careful aim, I fired the first barrel. The resulting shot caused the squirrel to fly off the side of the branch, hit broadside by the number six shot. As expected the other one leaped to a nearby limb at a full run for better cover and a short-term future not in Mama's kitchen. Making a quick move to the left to get a clear second shot my foot slipped off the wet tree root chosen earlier for stability. Down the hill, I crashed followed by a dangerously unreliable eight-gauge shotgun with one remaining live shell an inch away from one fickle, cocked hammer. Through the leaves we tumbled, stopping against the trunk of a hickory, me on my back, the shotgun barrel nestled snug against my throat. With no thought of attempting to move the gun, my hands at my sides were shaking to take action I couldn't allow. Recalling times in the past when one of the barrels went off without warning I lay perfectly still.

Like the voice of an angel Shorty said, "Don't move Mister Johnny, don't you move none boy."

Though his tone sounded angelic the words registered like a military order but from my perspective, a command to lie still wasn't necessary. Before I could blink he stood over me. In a split second, with one big hand, he knocked the shotgun clear from under my neck further down the side of the hill. There among the leaves pointing downhill lay the untrustworthy squirrel killer, the one hammer still cocked, ready to fire.

"I'm sorry, I didn't want to touch that ole gun tryin to move it away careful like. I was too afraid the old rascal might go off on you any second," he said, tears filling his eyes.

For the first time, I realized this man cared about me a lot. My body began moving faster than my mind could think grabbing hold of him as though he might be the last person to ever hold on to. The adrenaline kicked in, tears began to flow. Clutching him tight for a long time my appreciation for far more than saving me from the eight-gauge came out long overdue. I held on out of gratitude for all the things he had done for my family, for what he meant to us. Giving up all my wrong thinking about him came easier than expected. Never again did I refer to him as a Negro, realizing my way of using the label was a putdown. To me, the term did more than differentiate people of a particular race. It suggested a lesser class of person. Nothing could be more untrue about the man who had become my friend, the closest I would have again for a father. My thinking had been so horribly wrong.

Extra Chair for the Table

After my squirrel hunting episode with the eight-gauge, I asked Mama about Shorty eating with us, "Why can't we let Shorty eat inside with us? I know he goes to the barn since it's colder now, but the temperature isn't much better in there."

No doubt she recognized my attitude about him had changed since the day in the cemetery, not solely based on him pulling the shotgun off me. She smiled with soft eyes saying, "I don't mind where he eats. I feel the same as Grandpa Eddie and your Grandma Mattie. Shorty can eat wherever it suits him."

"Can I ask him then?"

"You ask him but let's respect his decision on it."

"Oh, and why does he always call us Miss or Mister all the time?" I added.

Considering thoughtfully before answering she said, "Well, why don't you ask him about that too?"

"Okay, but what do you think Mama?"

"There could be a lot of reasons but I think he's just trying to be polite. Black people have to always worry about how they act around white people but it's not the other way around. When the slaves were brought here from Africa all those years ago they were forced to act polite or else their white masters might treat them badly. They aren't slaves anymore but they still have to be careful around white people. There are white people who do horrible things to others, especially Negroes. Some whites feel better about themselves by treating black people poorly. It's pretty sad and makes no sense to me honey. We are all the same in God's eyes. Wrong thinking made slaves out of those people. Treating them or anybody else badly is wrong. You go ask Shorty. Tell him we would prefer he call us simply Emilie or Sara or Johnny, but let's leave the decision up to him."

She had given me a lot more than I bargained for or understood. The matter of white and black people getting along had always been complicated. But the problem began to seem mostly due to white attitudes. Being white created an immediate concern. Wondering what should be done, sorting out the matter in my mind, would take the rest of my childhood and longer. At the moment though, I had a mission. We hadn't had breakfast yet and, as usual, Shorty had begun working in the barn. Bent over next to Jane, he held one of her hooves off the ground, snug between his legs replacing a busted shoe.

"Good mornin Mister Johnny," he said looking up, "do ole Shorty a favor. Reach me the rasp while this here mule is standin good and still. I done lef it over in th tool bucket."

Nothing more than a large file with sharp teeth we used the rasp for trimming hooves. Handing over the tool he wanted, he gave me the nippers used to cut the hoof like nail clippers.

I jumped right into my planned conversation, "Shorty, Mama says you should eat with us inside. She says you should call her Emilie, not Miss Emilie, and stop calling the rest of us Miss or Mister."

My knack for being direct could often backfire if whatever said wasn't well thought out. Though the discussion with Mama hadn't gone exactly the same as the version I gave Shorty, putting a twist on it might convince him easier than just asking.

Never looking up, he continued to work on Jane's hoof when she shifted her weight, "Whoa mule," then, "How come she was to say somethin like that all of a sudden?"

Not wanting to give the impression she ever thought otherwise my strategy had to change right off the bat.

"Well, just because she never said anything until now doesn't mean she didn't think it."

"Then why is she bringin it all up today, this mornin?"

This wasn't going as I had hoped. An older kid would have known they were being played with but not this eight-year-old.

"Uh, well, I asked her about it but she said it was okay by her."

"Was you also jiss askin bout me callin her Miss Emilie?"

Never making eye contact proved he had no intention of making this easy.

"Well, I guess so, yeah."

Looking up he asked, "What zactly did you ask yer Mama?"

The entire discussion had become exasperating. "I don't see why you can't eat inside with us and I don't see why you have to call us Miss or Mister all the time."

Laying the rasp flat across the hoof he held it with a hand on each end pulling vigorously side to side filing to create a smooth edge for the hoof to fit against the new shoe. Next, with an abrupt move rehearsed many times between him and the mule, Shorty stepped to the right allowing her to drop the foot to the ground, shifting her weight to a preferred position.

Placing the rasp in the box with the other farrier tools Shorty walked over and put an arm around me, "Come over here and let me see if'n I can explain."

A wooden bench sat in front of Jane's stall midway inside the barn. More life lessons were learned sitting on that bench next to Daddy or Shorty than in all my years of formal schooling. It came to be known as the stool school.

Shorty sat down with me standing in front of him, "Some black people's think it's hard livin around whites. It ain't all that hard. They's a lot of things ain't fair for black folks and a lot of things we don't like but goin around all puffed up bein mad all the time don't do one thing to fix any of it."

This didn't seem to have anything to do with my questions requiring a heavy dose of concentration on my part to sort out.

He continued, "All the bad, unfair stuff been takin place for two or three hundred years in this country alone. I don't spect it's gonna get fixed no time soon. It took me a long time to come to but I finally decided if'n I was gonna get along I was gonna have to try extra special hard if'n I wanted to or not..."

Still not knowing where this would end up I said, "But what does all the bad stuff have to do with you eating with us or what you call us?"

"I'm gittin to it. A long time ago my pappy's pappy was owned by a white man over to the Benton Plantation with a hundred other black folks. When I was little he tolt me all the slaves had to call ole man Benton, Massa and the ole man's wife they had to call Miss Catherine. My grandpappy tolt me I didn't have to call nobody Massa anymore but for me to always be respectful to white and black folks alike if'n I wanted to get along in the worl. He done tolt me black folks keep out of trouble better the more they stays away from white folks. So I decided I could be respectful by sayin Miss or Mister to white folks. The other thing is I never in my life saw us black peoples sit down to eat with any whites which seemed like a good way to help keep me away from trouble."

My degree of paying attention was higher at the moment than ever in Mrs. Shelby's class. She taught us about the Civil War and slavery. Paying better attention back in school might have helped me understand what Shorty wanted to communicate. Here I stood talking to someone who not only had known a slave the fella had been Shorty's own grandpa. Like Mama said a few minutes before, Shorty told me much more about black people having to act a certain way around whites to get along. Slavery ended well over seventy-years ago causing me to think, shoot, white people are pretty hard-headed if all these years later they still make blacks feel the way Shorty described. Mama often called me hard-headed but maybe being white made understanding difficult for me. On the other hand, maybe Shorty and the other black folks he called peoples were a little hard-headed too.

Maybe they would all be better off just getting over it.

Something wasn't right though. Time and time again I had seen or heard how bad whites like the Harlows treated blacks while never once witnessing a black person treat whites badly. Shorty had brought up a lot to think about on an empty stomach, but I had to say something else wanting my message to come out strong, meaningful.

"Well, okay, I don't mean okay about the bad part. I mean okay I understand but none of those things matter around here. This is our farm and we can do things the way we want to. We want you to eat with us and not call us Miss or Mister," I said.

Considerably impressed with my response I placed both hands on my hips. He looked into my eyes for a long silent minute maybe trying to see all the way inside my head but instead saw inside my heart.

"Well, you sure yer mama said that's what she wants? You ain't foolin with me none are you?"

Beginning to shake my head no he continued, "No I believe you sho ain't foolin with me. I'd be quite pleased to take my food with yer family if'n that's what you all want. And I'll jiss call you boys by yer first names with no mister attached. But I ain't gonna quit callin yer mama Miss Emilie and I ain't gonna quit callin yer sister Miss Sara. They's womens and womens got to get more respect than mens do. I won't do it. You needn't think bout sayin any more bout it."

It felt like a major victory, but agreeing with the idea my sister Sara should have my respect would not happen in this lifetime. Heck, sometimes she punched me for saying or doing something she didn't like. Anyhow, having learned the term 'never ever' long before, 'never ever' totally getting my way, this would be no different. My smile could have been agreement enough but a handshake to seal the deal between us seemed more appropriate, official. Offering my outstretched hand Shorty smiled as well before swallowing mine inside his own with a gentle but firm grip. We shook once, then twice for good measure. Any difference in color between us vanished with my hand completely disappearing into his. It felt all kinds of good. Convincing him to eat inside with us gave me a good feeling. But knowing he liked me enough to take my hand felt better than anything else at the moment. After our handshake, he stood taking my right hand in his left. He held on all the way to our back door. Shorty's hands were bigger than Daddy's but holding mine reminded me of him.

With Shorty standing next to me inside the back door I announced our agreement. Mama tried to protest him continuing to refer to her and Sara as Miss but he said, "No Ma'am, I ain't gonna do it. I'll eat with you folks and be happy you want me too.

And I'll call these here boys Junior and Johnny and Wes. But you is Miss Emilie and this here young girl is Miss Sara. That's jiss the way it's gonna have to be."

Nobody ever stood their ground against Mama, not Sara or Junior or me or Daddy. Grandpa Eddie never tried. Every one of us kids, somewhat stunned, looked in silence at our mother for her response. Though gentle, kind and normally soft-spoken, we all knew better than to get on her bad side. Shorty stood, rolled his hat up into what looked like a suede rolling pin, otherwise unmoving, silent and waiting staring right into her eyes.

To our amazement, she said, "All right then, Johnny, Shorty can't sit at this table without a chair. We're gonna need another one. Get Daddy's chair."

The gloomy, mournful thundercloud hanging above our house every day since Daddy died moved away from blocking the sunlight. In no time the tension in the room went out the back door, across the yard right down to the lake. Mama had moved the chair into the corner to make more room at the table. Moving it back to the table made sense to me though someone different would be sitting there. We all sat in our regular places leaving Daddy's chair for Shorty but he hesitated, saying nothing.

"Well, sit down Shorty, what is it now?" Mama, beginning to seem somewhat put out, asked more of a question than a command to sit.

Still not taking a seat he said, "Ma'am, I think Mister, I mean Junior here should sit in his pappy's chair, him bein the oldest boy. I'll take his if'n you don't mind."

Junior looked over with eyebrows raised silently appealing for her agreement. Her look became gray and somber.

Sara said, "It's okay Mama. We can get one of the stools from the back porch. Wes won't mind sitting on it, will you Wes?"

Wes wasn't paying much attention until hearing his name called. He said, "What? I didn't do anything."

In the midst of Junior and me laughing she added, "No, I didn't say you did anything. I said you wouldn't mind sitting on a stool to let Shorty have your chair."

But Mama didn't laugh. She stood with one hand covering her mouth, perfectly still, her eyes looking at the floor, just blinking. A tear formed at the corner of one eye growing in size until it ran off her cheek.

"Awe Miss Emilie, I'll just eat out to the barn. You don't need to go to no fuss on my account. You let Mister William's chair stay right where it sits." Shorty said.

Removing the hand from her mouth and holding it palm out but shaking Mama said in a somewhat desperate tone, “No, wait. Sara, Shorty, all of you wait.”

We waited and we stared, even Wes could tell Mama was having a serious moment. Either she couldn’t decide what to do or this was one of many times she would have admitted to herself the reality of Daddy being gone forever.

After a long silence in a quiet, controlled voice she made a matter of fact comment looking at Junior, “I think Junior taking William’s chair is a fine idea.” After a pause to wipe the tear from her face she added, “You’re the man of this house now Junior. Thank you for being so thoughtful Shorty. Now, unless ya’ll want to eat cold biscuits you two need to get in your seats so we can say grace.”

Junior couldn’t contain himself jumping into his ‘man of the house’ chair. He sat beaming while Sara said grace. Though my eyes should have been closed, looking over at him couldn’t be avoided. His weren’t closed either as he gave me a smile of satisfaction.

First Hog

In between passing biscuits and the last pieces of ham from the previous fall, Mama and Shorty decided the weather would likely stay cold enough to slaughter a hog. The hog had to hang in the open air for a while. Any warm weather could ruin the meat. Plus the cold weather kept the flies away.

We killed a hog every fall which provided enough meat to get us through the year. The meat would be stored in a wooden bin in the smokehouse layered with salt to prevent spoilage while curing. After smoking the butchered meat, Daddy layered a few pounds on top of a fresh blanket of salt in the bottom of the bin, covered the meat with salt, added more meat plus more salt, layer upon layer filling the bin to the top. Smoked salt-cured ham is nothing like the sugar-cured meats the big packing houses produce today. I've tried ordering salt-cured ham with breakfast around different parts all over the country. People don't understand what I'm asking for outside of the south. They think it's the same as sugar-cured ham or smoked ham but it's not close. Once in a diner in Chicago, the waitress asked their cook who came over to my table.

He wanted to clarify what she had asked. After doing so he said, “Oh yeah, I know salt-cured ham, had it once. That stuff isn’t fit to eat.”

The comment didn’t surprise or insult me, I simply answered, “Well it’s whatever you get used to I suppose.”

Growing up we ate pig’s brains too. Mama canned the brains for storing, frying a few ounces in the mornings with bacon fat before sprinkling them on top of scrambled eggs. They looked similar to ground beef crumbled on top of the eggs except for the gray instead of brownish color. Not until becoming a teenager did the color of the meat make me curious. But complaining didn’t make sense after Mama explained the gray colored meat. We kids had been eating them all those years with our eggs.

Shorty could do anything needed around our farm, from planting to repairing equipment to caring for the animals. Mama asked if he could do the hog butchering with Junior’s help. Of course, in my mind, she hadn’t asked the right question. She should have asked with Junior’s ‘and’ my help. Daddy would never let us watch or help until we reached the age of ten which must have been a magic age close to manhood. Junior helped Daddy for the first time the previous fall. He said guttin a hog amounted to about the same as a big rabbit except hogs had a lot more guts. It didn't sound too bad to me, having seen plenty of rabbits and squirrels gutted, helping to clean those smaller animals at times.

So in the fall of 1933, the time had come for my first hog killin. Arguing to Mama she should allow an eight-year-old, who soon would be ten, to help, to my surprise she didn't mind. Apparently, Mama did plenty of things differently from Daddy which wasn't a surprise either. Once, after Mama and he argued about something or other Daddy told us kids how husbands and wives look at lots of things differently. He said when you marry somebody they become your life partner. He said you have disagreements with partners, but if you care about the person enough you work through the situation and move on with life.

He used a term called compromise. When asked what it meant he said, "You win some you lose some."

Maybe my older brother understood but from my point of view having a girl as a partner brought up all kinds of unimaginable, unpleasant outcomes. My sister Sara always had to have things her way. Evidently, she hadn't learned compromise yet. Merely a brother, no part of my being would have her or anyone like her for a partner. Having a partner who would punch me for looking at them the wrong way wasn't appealing in the least.

Junior reminded Mama of Daddy's age rule about helping with the hog slaughtering to which she responded, "I know but he's not here. You boys have to do these things now. It'll be okay."

Shorty never knew Daddy's rule on the subject. Anyhow, he would do whatever Mama wanted including her approving of Wes tagging along. I hadn't counted on Wes following me or Mama not saying something to stop either of us. Shorty got up first, followed by Junior. They got their coats, bundled up and went straightaway out the back door.

Trying not to give Mama any reason to think on it further, getting out the door for me required a quiet but quick move while she and Sara cleaned up from breakfast. The door hinges were rusty. Their screeching sounded ten times louder than usual. Easing the door closed I stepped down onto the single stone step into the cold crisp November air in our backyard. Safely out in the clear a test of the air confirmed what kind of day we were in for. Taking in a long breath and exhaling slowly, the warm air from my lungs froze, suspended, floating for an instant.

After no more than three steps the door hinges screeched again louder for what seemed like an eternity this time as Wes came running right behind me, the door slamming like the crack of a rifle.

Stopping him in his tracks I said, "You get back in the house. This ain't gonna be anything for kids to see."

"Mama said I could watch and I'm gonna." Pushing past me toward the hog pen Wes didn't flinch or slow down.

Going back inside to check out his story could result in me missing something. After hearing about this my whole life, the time had come at last for me to watch with the full expectation Shorty would let me help in some way. But Mama allowing a young kid like Wes to come out with us bigger boys didn't make sense for a job Daddy obviously felt better suited for grown men or, as in my case, practically grown men. Plus, not wanting my argument with Wes to draw any more attention to my own age, as long as he stayed out of our way it made sense to say nothing more.

We were there to do serious killing work which may have been a strange way to think about the job ahead of us, but it was, it was serious killing work. Well, for sure more serious if you were the hog. For the rest of us, the task meant having enough meat to get through the next year. This morning would indeed teach me how serious hog killing could be, not only for the hog. Literally gut-wrenching for anyone watching for their first time,

Wes would soon agree without ever saying a word. We stopped halfway across the yard thinking, rightly as the situation unfolded, we were close enough. Staying in my original spot may have been one of the best decisions of my life.

By the time we came to a stop, my eyes were wide opened and anxious. Shorty and Junior stood in front of the hog pen. The hog pen smelled worse than anything else on the place, maybe worse than anything else anyplace. Daddy built their pen across the yard next to the barn.

Pepper tagged right along as usual. Shorty's terrier never missed out on anything. Assuming they were going on an early morning squirrel hunt he ran circles around them all the way across the yard out toward the woods, stopped, looked back, and barked which must have meant, "Come on let's go."

But when we didn't the eager little dog ran back over every bit as enthusiastically to find out what the alternative plan was. Watching him often made me think being a dog would be the life. They never got disappointed over anything, got plenty of petting and someone always fixed food for them. Realizing Mama always fixed my food and the petting could get old, the major advantage would be never getting disappointed, which alone would still be a good enough reason to be a dog.

Shorty had made a quick detour on his way across the yard pulling our ax out of a piece of log next to the wood pile. What he might have in mind for the ax made for some gruesome pictures in my head. No doubt, our biggest hog, the object of Shorty's plan, would find out pretty quick and first hand.

All three hogs came over to the fence as if Shorty approached the pen carrying a slop bucket full of watermelon rinds. People never came over to them without bringing something to eat. We fed them everything we had from leftovers to rotten vegetables from the garden. They ate everything. We threw rotten apples picked up off the ground to kill horseflies on their backs. The hogs ate the apples though they were rotted something gross or had horsefly guts on them from the ones we nailed with a good throw. Hogs ate disgusting things and we ate them. I've eaten them all my life. Their system must clean up what they eat since their meat is the best a hungry person could ask for.

Junior stopped next to the gate while Shorty climbed over jumping in holding the ax close up on the handle next to the ax head itself. The hogs didn't pay any attention to him whatsoever. They rooted about as usual, innocently unaware a stranger stood in their midst in the pen. Pepper ran back and forth along the bottom row of chicken wire around the pen not barking but getting the hog's attention. He wanted to get in the pen with them. He most likely thought he knew how to help his master by creating a distraction, chasing them and barking constantly. The hogs were busy keeping an eye on the dog while, at the same time, rooting around on the ground for whatever we may have brought out for them to eat. Two of them were smaller, a year or two younger than the big one. This wouldn't be their day to die but the bigger one's final morning would have a quick, ugly ending.

Shorty walked up to the big hog from behind. With no hesitation, he raised the ax over his head with the blunt end pointing at the unsuspecting animal. Holding his weapon of choice high overhead Shorty had prepared to strike the hog with the blunt side of the ax. The steel ax landed square on the back of the big hog's head making a cracking sound as if a dry two-inch log had been snapped in two stepped on by a giant. The hog fell instantly, straight to the ground. The blow must have broken his neck or skull causing his legs to quit working. Neither of the other hogs had ever seen one of their pen mates killed before. They proceeded, in a matter of a few squeals, to get themselves as far away as possible on the other side of the pen. Looking back at the dead or dying hog, blood spurted up like a stream, thick and red settling on the ground around his head, painting the fence posts a deep blackish, red color.

Right about the same time the back door hinges screeched again. Wes had made his exit in a hurry going back in the house quicker than the other two hogs made their way to safety. If he squealed anything like the hogs I didn't notice. The situation required a quick decision from me as well, right on the spot. Wheeling to run like Wes would prove me too young, not yet close to being a man. Not choosing the option of running required me to stand my ground, acting as though the brutal event taking place in front of my eyes gave no cause for concern whatsoever. Over the recent fall seasons Daddy had answered all my questions providing all the gory details of hog slaughtering, but talking about it and witnessing the actual deed were two different things. At the moment though, the urge to lose my biscuits began to grow strong. But throwing up would be right up there at the top of the list of unmanly reactions, no better an option than running for the back door. Things were happening way too fast for this eight-year-old to make the kind of decision the situation called for.

While trying to make multiple critical decisions, all of which would affect everyone's perception of me for years to come, more things began happening inside the hog pen. Junior opened the gate helping Shorty grab the hog by its back legs. They began dragging the dead animal out into the backyard across to the tree where all large animals like deer or hogs were hung for butchering. Pepper positioned himself right at the gate making sure the other hogs stayed put while stealing opportunities to sniff the dead hog's head probably to make sure Shorty hadn't brought the huge creature out alive. This part wasn't too bad giving me the mistaken idea the rest of this couldn't be as bad as the actual killing itself. Animals hanging on the pulley and hook, with feet removed and bloodless ribs showing inside an empty cavity staring at us in the house, never bothered me in the least as they turned slightly back and forth on a windy day. One day they were animals, the next they were meat.

Nonetheless, my stomach seemed to agree with the decision to stay, to help from a safe distance, like the spot chosen before the bloody event began. But maybe Wes left in such a hurry because he somehow sensed what would happen next. Regardless, his decision to go back into the warm, safe house proved to be the better choice.

The air outside, unusually cold this particular morning, combined with my nervousness to give me a chill as the butchering began. My chosen spot for observing ended up being closer to the butchering than the hog pen allowing full view of every awful detail. Shorty's knife had been hidden deep in his pants pocket inside its leather sheath. Once they had the hog sufficiently raised off the ground with the hind legs close to the top Shorty made a quick cut around the hog's neck allowing all the remaining blood to drain out. After the blood spurting awfulness in the pen, the sight of more blood came as a surprise. Apparently, I had the wrong idea about how much there was in a big hog. Hot, thick red liquid covered the ground underneath the dead animal, steam rising into the colder air. Before the blood quit running from the gaping open neck wound Shorty made another cut down the middle of the belly.

An instantaneous, unbelievable smell created the last significant memory of my first hog butchering. Skin holding the guts in place began to spread open as if Shorty's blade had unzipped a thick skin sweater. A plume of steam filled the air accompanied by a smell ten times worse than holding your face over a pot of boiling meat. The foul stench floated on the breeze, which wafted, as luck would have it, in my direction. Overwhelming my senses, there were no similarities, in my mind, between this and gutting a rabbit or squirrel. It occurred to me throwing up right there, in the middle of the yard, in the middle of the butchering, might be okay after all. Certainly, anybody who ever encountered such things for the first time would likely lose their biscuits and molasses regardless if they were eight-years-old or forty-eight. My own stomach ached as though Shorty's knife had cut mine like the hogs. Within less than a minute, the contents of my own guts could be lying out on the ground like those across the yard which minutes before were firmly intact inside a living, breathing animal.

My pride wasn't sufficient to keep me there longer. Making my turn to the back door as painfully slow as possible in hopes of saving a shred of honor, escaping the slaughter and gore required measured yet quick steps across the still frosty grass. Maybe Shorty assumed me watching would be okay because his first hog butchering happened before the age of nine. The experience for this kid would be remembered a long time. Though never saying anything to Mama, she received the blame for allowing me to go out there. How could somebody as kind and gentle as her let a kid, though quickly approaching manhood, watch something as gruesome as a hog slaughtering?

With the door closed safely behind me, my stomach felt somewhat more normal once again with thoughts of my big brother coming to mind. He had grabbed the bleeding hog helping drag it across the yard, staying out there through the gutting process without throwing up. That's the kind of big brother I would be for Wes one day but not today. Maybe by the time we killed a hog next year my stomach would be as tough as the rest of me had already become. Wes would have a real big brother. The morning had not been a complete disaster after all.

Sara's Predicament

Once a year, Mama took us to buy new shoes in town. Before the Depression, the town had three dry goods stores, but we always went to the same place anyhow. Pearson's Dry Goods sat on the corner right next to the Bank of Holly Springs on Memphis Street. The store shared one common wall with the bank sitting across from the courthouse. Junior and I thought up plenty of schemes for robbers to cut a hole through Pearson's into the bank vault where the dry goods were displayed. It seemed a logical plan though no one ever tried it as far as we knew.

Most of the town's stores were on the square around the Marshall County Courthouse. We did business at Pearson's for the same reason we bought groceries from Watsons, credit. Many stores had gone out of business because the owners kept their money in banks other than the Bank of Holly Springs. Referred to by nearly everyone as the "hometown bank," it managed to remain one of few surviving in the state. We had cash money for the cotton crop by the end of November. Our new shoes didn't have to go on Mama's credit, but she bought other things there throughout the year paying them off later in the fall after the harvest.

The year was 1935. Whether my shoes had worn out or not didn't matter. At ten years of age, my feet had grown so much the past year the shoes didn't fit. We hardly wore them in the summer. When putting mine on to go back to school in September they crammed my toes together causing all ten to go numb after sitting for any amount of time. Mama said we would cut the end out of them if we had to which would help us get by until the cotton money came in. We were required to wear shoes for school, but when harvest time came we preferred going barefoot. The bottoms of our feet had become pretty tough plus my toes would have thanked me every day if they could talk.

The day for shoe shopping came right before Thanksgiving. Grandpa Eddie gave Mama a ride into town while my brothers and I walked the two miles in from school. After shopping, we would catch a ride home in the back of Grandpa Eddie's pickup. Riding in the open back of a pickup truck brought with it a kind of freedom. With the wind blowing in your hair everything passed by right in front of your eyes almost at arms-length, the roadway, fences, people, houses, on and on. Behind the truck, a trail of dust would billow up off the road creating such a dirt fog a person couldn't see or breathe in the road until it settled once again covering roadway, trees, and fields. Watching a pickup go by with a hound in the back, nose over the side into the wind but never offering to jump, created an impressive sight, a demonstration in self-government. Enjoying the cool wind bringing a million scents to its nose, the dog always chose life over jumping to its death. The first and only time I tried sniffing into the wind from the back of Grandpa's truck, one of those giant black wasps hit me square in the forehead falling right in my lap too dead to sting or do any more damage. Freedom can come with unthinkable risks.

Grandpa parked in the front as we walked up. We were up the steps going into the store before Mama got out of the truck. Junior stopped to hold Pearson's door open for her. Always doing those kinds of things caused me to wonder where he learned them. Thirteen now, maybe his age group had been taught in school how men should be toward women. On second thought, none of my uncles had mastered the art of being polite to women or their mama, Grandma Sara, which told me either my theory about learning it in school was wrong or else they just didn't listen very well.

Grandpa Eddie always took the opportunity to go across the street to a place called BJs to play pool and visit with his buddies. All the old guys, including a few younger ones, hung out there during the day especially after the crops were in sharing stories or telling lies about all kinds of things. The local news, which included plenty of hearsay, came from the pool hall. Grandpa got his real news from the South Reporter, Marshall County's newspaper or the Commercial Appeal from Memphis.

Mr. Pearson came from the back having stashed a bunch of boxes emptied after stocking his shelves. Seems every time we went into the store, he came to the front bringing along a familiar smell. It was similar to the smell on Daddy when he came in to tell us goodnight after playing cards with his brothers. The noisy front door opening and slamming signaled Mr. Pearson to walk to the front to greet Mama, "Hello Emilie, ya'll come on in here and get yourselves warmed up."

He didn't know if she had walked to town or not. The weather had become plenty cold outside. Mr. Pearson never married becoming awful nice to Mama after Daddy died. Junior said, in his opinion, Mr. Pearson wasn't Mama's type. Balding at an early age, he wore a hairpiece balanced precariously in a different place on his head every time we saw him. Junior didn't think his unruly fake hair had much to do with why he wasn't Mama's type but from my point of view could be reason enough. Of course, Mr. Pearson had plenty of money, but money never impressed Mama. How women made the decision about what type they liked became a curiosity for some time after my discussion with Junior.

A pot belly stove stood in the middle of the floor close to the wall where the sundries were displayed. Those were all manner of personal items like toothpaste, toothbrushes, lipstick for women and pomade for slicking down a man's hair. We decided Mr. Pearson should have used a couple of globs of his own pomade if it would help his wandering hairpiece stay in place. The sundry items were interesting to look at, but Mama never bought any of them. She said they weren't necessities which would be the last thing to get any argument from me. We preferred standing next to the wood stove while Mama shopped.

"I'm fine Mr. Pearson, Daddy drove me up today but you're right, it's unusually cold out." Mama, being respectful as always, must have felt she should call him Mr. Pearson instead of Elmer, his given name. He was at least ten years older than her.

"I suppose Mr. Daniels headed over to BJs to get himself caught up on the news and fine tune his pool game," he said.

"Yes sir, that's what Daddy claims anyhow. That's why he offers to bring me to town. By the smell of his breath afterwards though, there's more going on in there than news and pool."

Mr. Pearson took a quick step back saying, "You don't have to say sir to me Emilie and your daddy's a good man. I've never seen him drink more than a fella should. I bet he's never missed a day of work yet down at the Frisco."

By expressing the opinion Grandpa never drank more than he should, Mr. Pearson caused further discussion on the matter later between my brother and me. The old storekeeper himself had a reputation for having more to drink than a man should after closing his store for the evening not to mention those trips to his backroom during the day. Mama never liked all the drinking men did. They consumed plenty of alcohol on a regular basis, especially after the Depression started. Four-million men around Daddy's age had to go to the Great War which became known as World War I after the Second World War happened later in the 1940s. More than one-hundred-thousand of those men didn't come home from WWI. After the War, the Depression caused that same generation to lose their jobs and, all too often, everything they had. Other than some type of farming, people had little chance of making a decent living. Those men had plenty of reasons to give up, to stay drunk all the time. It's hard to think about how those desperate times affected them and the women too. They were all just in their early twenties during World War I only to have the economy fall apart in their thirties, realizing they would be in their forties or older before things got better.

In all honesty, though, plenty of alcohol got consumed on a regular basis before the Depression ever happened. Going back to the Prohibition years in the early 1920s when the Federal government outlawed the sale of alcohol plenty of folks began making their own liquor. They kept right on providing for themselves as well as selling some to other folks after drinking alcohol became legal again.

Mama got quiet while looking over the overalls lying out on a display table, picking up various sizes and holding them as if to get an idea how long they might last or how they would look on us.

Finally, she answered him, "You may be right about Daddy, I guess, but there's nothing good to come out of a bunch of men drinking in the middle of the day. Are you hearing any good news about the economy?"

"Not really. I'm sure you know Jacob Gurley, the new manager at the bank. He came in the other day to buy pipe tobacco. He says banks are closing all over the country. Over four thousand have gone out of business. Our bank is holding its own like a handful in every state, but people in other parts of the country are losing everything they had. The main reason me and Charlie Watson have been able to keep our stores open is we kept our money hid away in cash or in the Bank of Holly Springs. That's about the only reason we can continue to offer good folks like you credit to get you through the year. Of course, I'd find some way to help you out anyhow Emilie. Yeah, it's pretty bad out there."

He continued, "And I hear it's worse in the big cities. Those city folks don't have any place to grow their food or raise a pig. President Roosevelt started this program called the CCC which stands for Civil Conservation Corps. They're takin hundreds of thousands of young men from the cities, sending them all over the country to work for the government building bridges as well as cabins in all those new state parks. They're plantin trees all over. He's payin em twenty-five dollars a month, but they can't keep more than five dollars. They have to send the rest back home to help out home folks. It's a pretty popular plan, but it's gonna take a lot more to get things going again if you ask me."

Junior and I stood listening around the edges of Mr. Pearson's comments. Parts of it made sense convincing me living in our country had become difficult especially for anyone not living on a farm. We had tough enough times on the farm, but other folks were having their own troubles. The conversation between Mr. Pearson and Mama convinced me things weren't good anyplace in our country causing me to wonder how the Depression began in the first place.

Mama said, "That's what I've heard from people on Sundays at church too. We do appreciate you and Mr. Watson for helping us out during the year. But today I want to make a payment for what we owe and these boys need new shoes. I'll bring Sara back another day. She doesn't need shoes this year. Her chores are mainly inside around the house but regardless she isn't near as hard on shoes as these boys. She's not growing as much anymore either. Besides she would rather have a dress than shoes."

To us, she said, "Boys get on over by the shoes so Mr. Pearson can measure your feet."

To the store owner, she added, "And you may as well fit them with something a size bigger than they measure for. They are all three growing faster than I can get my cornbread cooked. I for sure don't want to have to buy more shoes before next fall. No offense to you."

"I understand completely, no offense taken. By the looks of those boys you cook a pretty good skillet of cornbread Emilie," he answered with an ear to ear smile.

Mama must have known the man wanted an invite but she wasn't a Cook fish taking the Pearson bait. She said, "Well, that's mighty nice of you to say Mr. Pearson."

With her eyebrows raised, she said nothing more. The ensuing silence sent a clear message to the old guy. Turning to us he said, "come on boys let's see how big those feet are this year."

Things were going as they had year after year for us, but Sara's day would be a lot different. Mama asked her to meet us at home. She was told to get dinner started. Usually, we walked home from school together. The high school and our middle school were next to each other. But sometimes Sara stayed later to work on a special assignment with a teacher. She started her first year of high school in the fall, the smartest of all of us, without question. She was also the hardest working by far at getting an education. On her way home though, something happened none of us will ever forget. She told Mama and the rest of us as soon as we got home.

The walk home went beside the old highway turning off onto dirt roads for the last two miles. All the property along those dirt roads, including one actual road, belonged to Grandpa Lewis until you reached our farm. No other families had homes along there. Cotton fields, hay fields or horse pasture stretched as far as you could see in any direction. We walked those roads day after day without seeing a single person unless a truck went past on the way to or coming from Grandpa's farm.

Sara heard a horse galloping up from behind as she made the last turn off the road into our driveway. As the rider came closer she recognized the troublemaker Sam Harlow. The Harlow's reputation went with them everywhere.

She said he trotted his horse right beside her, stopped, leaned down, and said, "Hey there Sara Cook. What are you doin walkin home all by yourself?"

She told Mama later the question, including his tone, convinced her right away he had trouble in mind. She said to him, "I walk home by myself sometimes, especially when my brothers come home before me."

"Well, I suppose you didn't today," he said.

She said she picked up her pace a little. Not wanting to engage him in any conversation she let his comment pass with no response.

"I see you walked home by yourself, but I don't believe the part about your brothers coming home before you." Sam insisted on pressing his point.

"How do you know what my brothers did or didn't do today? Besides, what business is it of yours anyway?"

"Well, I guess today you walked home before them."

Now she began to get concerned. She decided to lead him along while moving toward the house saying, "How do you know Sam Harlow? What difference does it make to you whether I did or not?"

"Oh, I saw those brothers of yours go into Pearson's Store with your mama a little while ago. I reckon you must be ahead of them today."

Continuing along her way she said over her shoulder, "So, I still don't see why you're bringin it up?" Once again trying to put him on the defensive she added, "And what are you doing out this way anyhow? You don't live around here, are you going to my grandpa's about something?"

His response proved the troublemaker had bad intentions. "Oh no, I ain't got no business with Mr. Cook. I wanted to come by to see you. You sure look pretty today."

Nudging the horse to speed up a little with a squeeze of his knees he began making up the distance between them as she got closer to the house. As the horse came up closer, almost bumping into her, she decided to try one final time to dissuade him verbally.

Stopping to face him she said, "Sam, I'm not even sixteen until next month. You're nineteen or twenty. You need to turn your horse around and leave." She tried being firm hoping not to insult or make him angry.

"Oh, I'm not all that much older. How bout I come inside for a while."

She told Mama she got scared after he said that. Practically to the house, she made a quick turn to the front porch saying over her shoulder, "You git yourself on away from our place Sam. You're not welcome. You're for sure not coming in. It's cold out here and I'm going inside."

As she stepped up onto the porch, to her horror, she heard him getting off the horse, the saddle scrunching leather against leather. A quick look back confirmed him on the ground running toward her. She said all she could think of was getting inside to lean against the door. Nobody bothered locking doors in those days, besides the lock on our front door didn't work. Slamming the door behind her, she leaned hard against the inside with all her weight hoping he would go away but fully expecting him to throw himself against it. What he did next surprised her.

Stopping outside the door Sam said, "Awe Sara, don't be like that. I only wanted to come in for a visit."

"Please, go away," she said.

It got quiet for a minute. Being heavier, he could push her away from the door with little effort. The old planks on the front porch creaked from the weight of his steps as he walked away from the door stepping off into the yard. Continuing to lean hard against the door she held her breath listening for the horse to move, but no sound came from the front yard. She told Mama she stood there thinking about all the times she had been told about being careful not to get in a place alone around grown men, especially one she didn't trust.

The hinges creaked as the back screen door opened followed by the door. Looking across the room into the kitchen she saw Sam standing in the doorway. She tried to go out the front door which required stepping back into the room closer to him to open the door giving him time to grab her arm above the elbow. She said she tried to pull away, but he held on so tight it began to hurt. Turning her head away she screamed, fighting as best she could, yelling at him while he tried pulling her close to kiss her. Stronger than her, Sam held her arms down at her sides.

"Now you better git yourself on away from that girl, boy." It was Shorty.

He told Mama he had been working in the barn when Sara screamed. Coming in the back door, he got Daddy's eight-gauge pointing the shotgun right at Sam's mid-section. The troublemaker stopped in his tracks.

Slowly letting go of Sara, Sam smiled saying, "Oh, you're the old Negro I saw with those Cook boys a few months back. I guess they did buy you. I never did..."

"You sho don't need to say nothin right now boy, you jiss needs to be gittin on away from here. This here eight-gauge is mighty ole and these ole hammers jiss have a mind of their own goin off when they wants to. Miss Sara, you come over here next to Shorty." Shorty said.

Shorty cocked both hammers on the shotgun. Sara said she moved the few short steps between her and Shorty as quick as she could stopping close behind him.

Sam raised an open palm as if to block anything coming from the barrel of the gun saying, "Now, you better point that shotgun someplace else old man. You ain't gonna shoot me cause if you do you know what'll happen to you."

Sam began moving his right hand as if to retrieve the knife from a leather scabbard on his belt.

"I ain't thinkin bout me right this minute boy, I'm jiss wondering how long I can hold this ole gun here before one of these hammers goes off by itself. It'll make some kind of terble mess outa you at this distance. If'n yer hand gits any closer to the pig sticker there on yer belt this here is gonna go real bad for you. Have you seen what a big shotgun will do at this distance? Now, I ain't gonna tell ya agin to git on away from here."

Sam's other hand felt for the door handle behind him without taking his eyes off the man holding the gun across the room.

Going through the doorway he said, "You ain't heard the last of this Negro. I'll see you another time. You'll wish you never pointed a gun anywhere near me."

They listened as the horse went first at a trot followed by a full canter out the drive to the road. Sara told Mama she began to cry.

Shorty said, "Come here honey, let ole Shorty hold on to you. He ain't gonna bother you now, come here."

She said her body shook all over something terrible, but Shorty held her tight for a long time not letting go until the shaking stopped. He stayed inside with her until we all got home saying he wouldn't leave her alone. At first, after Sara told her story, Mama said we should get Sheriff Barton immediately.

But Junior spoke, "Mama, Sam Harlow will lie to the Sheriff making trouble for Shorty. All a black man has to do is look the wrong way at a white man. We hear about it happening all the time. They'll lynch him for pointing a gun at Sam. I'll take care of this myself."

"You'll do no such thing, William Cook," she said.

Before she could say anything more Sara said, "Mama, let's leave it alone. Sam looked plenty scared going out the door. I don't think he'll come back around here. I don't want to make trouble for Shorty. I'm okay, really."

Shorty stood silent, willing to accept whatever fate came from the family's decision. After staying quiet for a long time Mama said to everyone, "Okay, I'm willing to keep this among us for now, but if there is a hint of anything else out of Sam Harlow or any of them Harlows I'm going to the Sheriff."

Junior added, "You won't have to do anything. I'll take care of it myself. I'm sorry, but I don't care what you say. I'll do it."

Mama didn't respond again to Junior but thanked Shorty several times. His working in the barn when Sara got home had been her good fortune.

Junior had a question, "How did you get the eight-gauge and get it loaded so quick Shorty?"

The hero of the day looked back and forth to everyone before saying, "I jiss grabbed me the big gun outta the kitchen corner from behind the door when I come in the back."

"But how did you find the shells to get the gun loaded so fast," Junior asked.

"That ole gun weren't loaded. I jiss pointed the barrel and cocked those hammers back. There weren't time to look for no shells. That boy didn't know the shotgun was empty. I spect if'n I was lookin down the barrel of an eight-gauge and somebody jiss tolt me the cocked hammers couldn't be trusted the last thing on my mind would be if'n it were loaded."

Regardless of the tense, somewhat frightful atmosphere, all we kids laughed. Mama smiled too. Sara went over giving Shorty another big hug with a kiss on the cheek which embarrassed him. It made me wonder for a while how a squirrel felt with an eight-gauge pointed at him.

Looking at Junior I said, “That Sam Harlow is as dumb as he looks.”

Mama corrected me for talking bad about somebody, even Sam Harlow who didn’t deserve any other kind of talk. Not until years later did I realize how Shorty’s quick thinking saved his own life while coming to Sara’s aid. Without threatening her attacker with the shotgun he would have had to take him on by hand. He would have had no problem handling the puny troublemaker. But laying his hands on a white man would have resulted in Sam’s family, accompanied by some other bad whites, coming after him for sure. Though neither Sara nor Shorty got hurt physically, the encounter with Sam wasn’t the last any of us would experience. Sam Harlow may have been dumb but later made good on his threat.

Thanksgiving at Grandpa Lewis'

Things got back to normal shortly after the Sam Harlow episode. Of course, Mama insisted Sara always walk home accompanied by her brothers which required us to wait for her at the high school on occasion. Admittedly, any time I buy shoes I'm reminded what our family went through over the Sam Harlow incident. Though certainly not understanding how serious the result could have been, he obviously had no good intentions. Junior got mad as a hornet staying mad for weeks. He said it would make more sense to me one day. He went on to say the episode made him mad as Hell which gave me reason enough to drop the subject. Words like Hell never came out of his mouth except for referring to things about the Bible or God which convinced me my brother must have been pretty awful angry.

The next week, Thanksgiving, we spent at Grandpa Lewis and Grandma Sara's. Mama didn't go. Shorty drove her in the wagon to our other grandparents place before coming back to Grandpa Lewis'.

I overheard Grandma Sara say to Grandpa, "That girl is welcome in this house like anyone else."

He said, "I never said she couldn't come here. I don't care one way or the other what she does or doesn't do."

"You don't have to say a thing, Lewis Cook. Your actions speak plenty loud enough for everybody to know what you're thinkin." Grandma ended the conversation.

Apparently, there was nothing else Grandpa Lewis could say. They didn't know I overheard their conversation. Grandma Sara started the discussion with Grandpa just after we arrived which indicated they were referring to Mama since she didn't come with us. Sara came with us boys which told me they for sure weren't talking about her. Guessing the entire thing had something to do with the issue between my grandpas once again I was reminded to get Mama to talk about it someday. Neither Sara nor Junior knew the particulars either so it would have to come from Mama.

Grandma Sara got along better with our sister than any two people ever could. Maybe having the same name had something to do with it, but whenever we went over there we wouldn't see our sister all day unless we went into the kitchen where she, Grandma and my uncle's wives were always cooking or cleaning up after feeding everybody. Of course, not seeing Sara all day didn't concern me in the least. The best way for me to stay out of trouble with her was to stay away. Later on, in the evenings the two of them would sit together, Grandma teaching Sara how to sew or knit; all those girl things. Meanwhile, unless we had terrible weather, Junior, Wes and I would be out around the horses or at the lake fishing or swimming.

We always had about ten cousins to play with on holidays. Two or three of us had the name Will or Johnny or Wes. Anyone named after a relative usually had a nickname. We had three girl cousins who stayed inside. But not Cousin Elizabeth, Uncle Johnny's oldest daughter, the same age as me. She didn't like any kind of girl stuff, but none of my cousins made fun of her. Though skinny as a rail, she could beat up about any boy which she did on more than one occasion. Everybody called her Lizzie. She must have been okay with the nickname or else I would have gladly called her whatever she wanted. Nothing could be worse than getting beat up by a girl your same age. We all went into the barn with the horses to get out of the cold. The heat all those horses put off made the barn almost as warm as our house with the wood stove burning all it could hold. Besides, Grandpa's barn made the perfect place to play hide and seek.

As the youngest of all the cousins, we let Wes be "it" first. This made the game go longer as he wasn't too good at finding us. Wes being too scared to climb the ladder made the loft a perfect hiding place. No sooner had I quietly situated myself behind a stack of hay bales than Lizzie ran in sitting right next to me. Holding a finger to her mouth for me to shush, we sat quietly listening to Wes counting before making the standard announcement,

"Ready or not, here I come."

He had no chance of finding us up there, but we stayed quiet, otherwise saying he heard us counted the same as finding us with his eyes. Once in a while, I looked over at Lizzie. Her soft breathing quickened with excitement for the game as she stared straight ahead listening. Maybe the game excited her or maybe just the idea of being found while in hiding. She glanced back at me and smiled. We had been outside for quite a while when my sister announced from the back door Grandma had dinner ready. A bale of hay hid us from the front. Our backs were to the barn wall with more bales on one side next to me. Lizzie sat unmoving on the other side blocking my exit. One of our other cousins answered Sara's call to dinner. In no time a commotion of voices commenced accompanied by the sound of feet shuffling through the dirt as they all headed out of the barn running to the house. But again Lizzie didn't move.

"Lizzie, let's go, Sara said dinner is ready."

Not answering, she looked at me with a wide-eyed smile.

I began again, “Lizzie, what...”

Given no chance to finish the sentence and without warning my cousin leaned over planting a kiss right on the side of my face. She jumped up quick heading for the ladder, starting to go down, before there was any chance to think about how to react.

I yelled, “Lizzie Cook, what in the world did you do that for.”

More than a mere surprise, a kiss coming from my cousin, even on the cheek, shocked the heck out of me. She stopped at the top of the ladder looking back saying, “If you tell anybody I’ll say you’re lyin and beat you til you can’t hardly walk.”

Beginning to make her way down again she paused once more to add, “And you won’t get any more of my kisses either if you tell.”

The first threat about getting beat up unnerved me, but the part about no more kisses didn’t seem like any kind of threat at all. Adding a manufactured smile, including an overdone wink, she proceeded to the ground. Thinking through what she said took a minute or so. Not the part about getting beat up; without a doubt she would do it. But making sense out of why she would kiss her own cousin beat up my brain more than she could beat up my body.

Grandma, our Aunts, Sara and the other girl cousins had made dinner which included the best pies for dessert, enough for all nine adults including fourteen kids with plenty of leftovers. Grandma made the best chocolate pie. All the adults were married except Uncle Wesley. The youngest of Daddy's brothers, at twenty-four, Wesley still lived with my grandparents. Grandpa said grace thanking God for everything except being unhappy God took Daddy too soon. Grandma always pinched his arm when he added any complaints reminding him God didn't need to hear him bellyache about anything including my Daddy dying young. Grandpa disagreed but we never heard him win an argument with Grandma. Most times he just went silent.

Pastor Carter tried to teach us God wanted to hear our complaints too, but after the way my sister tore in to me when I complained to her, the thought of what God might do prevented me from grumbling at Him any way shape or form.

No one knew what Grandpa thought after being corrected though it happened a lot, but only by Grandma. He never made any effort to defend himself which meant either an admission of guilt or else a complete denial of any wrongdoing. Regardless, neither of them said anything more about the prayer. The adults began filling plates for us kids before passing food around the main table.

Not having enough room at the table my aunts fixed places around the living room for the kids. Lizzie waited until I picked a good spot beside the fireplace. Holding a plate overflowing with dressing, gravy, sweet potatoes with a big turkey drumstick, she stood next to the table glancing over once in a while for me to get settled. Thankfully, she didn't want her intentions made obvious to anyone else. Knowing I wouldn't dare get up to move she sat down, giving me a smile, saying nothing.

All I could think to do was shake my head whispering, "Lizzie, what in the world?"

She whispered back, "You know you're my cutest cousin Johnny Cook."

Wanting to avoid anyone overhearing this crazy conversation I said, "Fine, let's just drop it."

Never looking up from her plate she smiled going for a fork full of sweet potato casserole. After dinner, the men always went outside to smoke or chew tobacco. Grandma didn't allow smoking inside. She told my uncles on a regular basis if they got caught spitting their nasty tobacco in her house, even into a can, she would beat them with a stick. She never went after anyone as far as I can remember but none of them broke the rule either, at least not with her around. My uncles apparently believed her threat though they were all grown. The same tobacco rules applied to Grandpa Lewis as well.

Usually, the kids went back to our own games outside. This placed me in a somewhat unsettling situation. My female cousin had sat through dinner giving me her undivided attention including a wink once in a while when she thought no one would notice. Uncle Wesley saved me though.

On the way out the back door he said, "Hey, you kids come out here and look at what I've got."

It didn't take me any time to run for the door. Unfortunately, Cousin Lizzie followed right behind me, but nothing like kissing your cousin could happen around all those grownups.

From inside a small outbuilding, my uncle brought out a caged baby raccoon. Sometimes people would catch one after killing the adults, but Uncle Wes said he found this one walking by itself across a newly harvested cotton field.

Uncle Wesley reached in carefully taking the young coon out of his cage saying, "Ain't he a cute little fella? Come on kids, you can all pet him."

Everybody wanted to pet him including Lizzie who had convinced me she had other things on her mind. My other uncles came over too. There must have been a dozen people watching the raccoon show. Maybe our crowd of people scared it or else somebody did something because without warning the baby raccoon started squirming to make his escape. Purely as a reflex, Uncle Wesley tightened his grip which caused the raccoon to bite him so hard the animal's teeth went all the way through his hand. The raccoon hung on for dear life. A raccoon would take on an entire pack of coonhounds at once biting the first dog through whatever part was first presented to it, never letting go until the other dogs killed him. This coon may have been a baby, but wild animals learn about protecting themselves long before they get grown.

Uncle Wesley began shaking his hand to get the raccoon loose yelling to his brothers or anyone who might be in listening distance, "Choke him boys, choke the son-of-a-bitch."

Blood flew around going everywhere either from my uncle's hand or the raccoon or both. Adults and kids alike were running everywhere while the bloody situation unfolded. Grandpa's house offered the safest place where neither the wild raccoon, nor cousin Lizzie was, at least for the moment. The animal's fate wasn't good, but the fate of Uncle Wesley's hand had plenty of question marks too.

We spent the rest of the afternoon inside playing Monopoly. At first, Lizzie laid on the floor right beside me but didn't bother to move after I got up to go to the other side. Lucky for me, she didn't wink once during the game except for when she landed on Boardwalk. She had bought Park Place earlier on beginning to organize her money to buy houses. Her actions from the barn continued to mystify me. Hopefully, she had lost interest in me though admittedly the attention wasn't bad, just the kissing part.

Later on, right before time to go home, we went back out again when the men went for another smoke. Hanging around adults meant listening to stories, which could be pretty boring but were sometimes filled with interesting experiences we looked forward to once we got older. Junior and I, with a couple of our boy cousins, were out there this time. Grandpa asked Uncle Johnny to bring out Grandpa's bitch coonhound Judy. Twelve years old and in poor health the old dog came out moving slow led by Uncle Johnny with Shorty and Calvin close behind. Another black man, Calvin worked for Grandpa. Grandma Sara served Calvin and Shorty Thanksgiving dinner out in the shed where Calvin worked. They weren't allowed to eat with white people at Grandpa Lewis's. The subject never came up. Grandpa Lewis' idea of how people should live around each other hadn't changed a bit from the way people thought in the 1860s. Growing up in the 1870s and 1880s the old way of thinking had, unquestionably, stuck with him for reasons difficult to understand. Meanwhile Grandpa Eddie, who grew up during the same years, had different ideas on those same subjects.

A Blue Tick Coonhound true to the breed, Judy's spots were such a pitch black color you would swear they were dark blue. Solid black fur surrounded her eyes with two tiny brown spots right above the eye. She had solid brown patches around the nose. Still more light brown covered the parts of her legs where she had no black flecking. Around her muzzle, the black and brown fur had long ago turned silver-grey, earned by twelve years of hunting and simply growing old. Long solid black ears flopped forward at each side of her face. Grandpa asked my uncles if they thought he should take Judy out to shoot her. Her face too had gone greyish silver. She carried her head hung low to the ground. Without question, the old dog felt poorly.

Having known her my entire life convicted me right away how horrible the idea of shooting her sounded. "Grandpa, you can't shoot Judy."

That put an end to all the talking. The adults, as well as the kids, looked at me at the same time.

Grandpa knelt down calling me over, "You like Judy don't you? I do too boy. She had the best nose of any coon hunter I've ever had but she's sick. When a dog gets as old as she is most times they can't get well. We don't want her to suffer do we?"

Everything said made perfect sense but still didn't matter to me. Continuing to protest I offered to take the dog home to try getting her to perk up but Junior butted in saying Mama wouldn't have it.

Shorty said, "Mister Lewis, sir, I'd be glad to take this here ole dog to see if'n I can do anything to make her get better. I promise you I won't let her suffer. I would never do such to an animal."

Turning to me he said, "I's agreein with yer Grandpa. We can't let this ole girl suffer not after all she's done givin Mister Lewis, you and everybody else. But if'n he's willin I'll doctor on her a while. We ain't lost nothin but a little bit of time. Mister Lewis, if'n I can get her well I'll bring her back over here to you straight away."

Grandpa considered the offer for a minute. Getting no comments either way from my uncles he asked Shorty, "You think you can get her on her feet?"

"I don't know sir but I believe I can keep her comfortable if'n she don't get well right away. She got nothin to lose sir. I can sho promise you I won't let her suffer none."

Grandpa silently studied further on the offer before answering. He loved his dogs whether they were a purebred coonhound or one of several mixed breed curs who had the job of lying on the front porch announcing the arrival of anybody who came to visit.

He said, "I tell you what. If you can get her through this you can have her as a gift."

"Mister Lewis, sir, I ain't askin for no gift."

"No, I don't believe you are. But old Judy would be grateful for another winter or two to run down some coons. If you can give her a few more good hunts I'm willin to let you have her."

Without question, Grandpa believed black people had a certain place or position in life which wasn't the same as whites. On the other hand, he could be generous. Regardless if you were white or black, you would get fair treatment if he liked you, at least his version of fair.

Looking over at Shorty it seemed a good time for me to put another two cents worth in. "I'll help you every day. You tell me what to do. I'll help you get her well."

Grandpa Lewis held out his hand to Shorty. Never before had he offered his hand to a black man, at least in front of me. He never did afterward to my knowledge. Shorty hesitated for a second, wiped his clean hand on the back of his trousers, and took Grandpa's, shaking on the deal. Shorty agreed to doctor on Judy. In exchange, Grandpa agreed he could have her as a gift. The deal they struck would be one of the best ever made over a dog.

World Class Coon Hound

Judy's recovery took several weeks but recover she did. Shorty fed her leftover table scraps we brought from our own table at the end of each day. He made a kind of greasy soup by adding water to a skillet full of nothing more than leftover biscuit gravy. Usually, Mama saved every bit she could, but she understood our mission. Being a dog person herself, she decided letting go a bowl of leftover gravy each day wasn't going to starve the rest of us. Sara brought an old blanket to keep Judy warm. Wes came to Shorty's with me once in a while to pet her on the head. She had more care than sick humans get. The first few days she barely lapped any of her soup, hardly responding, but sometime right before Christmas began walking around Shorty's cabin, circling and settling eventually with her back to the warm fireplace. Pepper would go over curling up next to her to nap.

After a while, she began following her new master all over the place. The gangly, awkward looking coonhound alongside the trim, pointy-eared terrier made for quite an interesting duo every place

Shorty went. Grandpa Lewis saw Judy with Shorty at our place one Sunday on his way home from church. Grandma came in for a short visit, but Grandpa would never come inside after Daddy died. The best I can remember he never came inside before, staying in his pickup or else visiting with us in the barn. A particularly cold day shortened their visit by offering a good excuse since he never wanted to stay long.

When they got ready to leave, Grandma and him in the truck, we all congregated around to say goodbye. Mama came no farther than the front porch. Grandpa said goodbye to her though he never told her hello when they arrived. This apparently showed his version of courtesy to her. Junior said if he had to guess, Grandma insisted Grandpa be courteous to Mama. Shorty stood at the corner of the house with his dogs. Pepper stood next to him while Judy sat watching her old master in the pickup, her head raised, staring as if wondering whether she should go to him or stay with Shorty. Grandpa put his window down calling over to him.

Shaking his head in disbelief he said, "I be damned Shorty. I sure thought the old girl was a goner. After she gets her full strength back you take the boys down in the bottom. Show them how good a coonhound she is. She is World Class Shorty, World Class."

With that, he spat a long string of tobacco chew out onto the frozen lawn and wiped the corner of his mouth with one of his many handkerchiefs.

Smiling back at him Shorty answered, "Yes sir, Mister Lewis, I will sho do it. I sho will. She's bout ready now but we'll give her plenty of time. We'll take her out right after Christmas."

Junior and I had been on a few coon hunts but never got to do more than sit around a fire listening to scary stories while the dogs hunted. The hunt we went on with Judy in early January can be called, without question, the coon hunt of a lifetime. First, we were going out on what must have been the coldest night ever since the beginning of record keeping in northern Mississippi. We had a NuGrape Soda thermometer on the wall right outside the back door which registered a ridiculous 5 degrees. The wind whipped about in such a frenzy the tree cover deep in the woods wasn't sufficient to keep us the least bit comfortable. Shorty came to our place not long after dark. Mama had us bundled up with what must have been every piece of clothing we owned to the point we could barely move, let alone walk. She told us to make sure we listened to him. She told Shorty to keep us as warm as possible.

Promises were made. Off we went to the bottomland on Grandpa Lewis' place, Junior carrying the eight-gauge this time, me following behind with an oil lantern. Shorty led with a second lantern. Pepper had to stay back tied at his cabin. A full-grown raccoon will kill a large coon dog not to mention a small terrier. Even though there wasn't a raccoon in the county fast enough to catch Pepper, the terrier's incessant barking could mess with Judy's hunt. Shorty had her on a long sturdy leather lead. She knew all too well what it meant. The leash, combined with going out at night, gave her all the clues necessary. She pulled on the leash with all she had, digging her front paws into the ground to pull harder, choking and coughing, as we headed across our front yard to the road. The long, freezing walk to the bottom, though less than a mile from our house, gave Junior and me more than enough time to rethink the idea of a coon hunt. The two kerosene lanterns we took for light provided nothing in the way of heat.

After crossing a small empty cotton field, we made our way down a slope into the woods. A creek ran through the middle of this part of Grandpa's woods which flooded the bottom at least every third spring with no more than a few inches of water but nonetheless covered every acre. The bottom consisted of more than four hundred acres. People referred to low lying land as bottomland. Often excellent for crops, but clearing this particular bottom didn't make sense as no amount of forecasting could determine which year the water might come up. Grandpa used the bottom for nothing more than timber cutting or hunting. Among the best of northern Mississippi's hunting properties, Grandpa, his buddies, along with my uncles killed plenty of deer in those woods every year. Once Junior turned twelve he got invited too. He came home afterward telling me his time with the older guys and Grandpa in the hunting shack in the middle of the bottom had been the best ever. Each year anywhere from twelve to fifteen men with a handful of teenage boys spent a week at the deer camp. Unless you were a terrible shot, you would come home with a deer.

Only the privileged few got to participate in the deer camp. If you were a good friend of Grandpa Lewis or else if you were kin and old enough you might get an invite. The same cast of characters usually went with the addition of any grandson once they reached the magic age of twelve. Before we were twelve, Grandpa allowed us to go during the fall for the coon hunts, which were not overnight affairs. But experiencing the mystique of deer camp first required coming of age, literally. A stickler for rules meant asking him to go on the hunt before your twelfth birthday would be useless. One year, our cousin Jimmy turned twelve two weeks after deer camp but still wasn't allowed to go until the next year. With Grandpa, rules were rules, not to be broken.

This night though, we had the bottom all to ourselves. Shorty found a bare spot next to the creek instructing us to gather sticks while he found large stones to build a makeshift fire ring. Judy couldn't stand the waiting, beside herself wanting to hunt, whining and carrying on. She wasn't allowed to go until we had a pretty good fire going to keep us warm. The fire building delayed her hunt, but otherwise, we would be left sitting in the cold while she hunted an hour or more before finding a coon. Once we had the fire cracking and popping Shorty unhooked the leash. At first, she ran about seeming to stretch her legs. She stopped, circling around for a big crap as if to relieve herself of any extra weight in preparation for a lot of running over the next couple of hours.

When Shorty began talking to her, her enthusiasm grew into a whining, barking, wiggling frenzy, "Come on Judy, coon, coon, hunt Judy, go find a raccoon girl."

Never stopping to look up at him she disappeared into the night woods to do her new master's bidding. Not a particularly big dog as coonhounds go, Shorty said we would need to get to her quick when she treed because a big raccoon could handle several dogs at once.

For my part, the cold became nearly intolerable, but the small fire improved things somewhat, at least if we got close enough. Shorty said we couldn't let the fire get too big to put out easily once Judy began to bay. Working on a plug of chewing tobacco stuffed into his cheek, he tried to convince us smoking couldn't be healthy adding it also didn't allow your hands to stay free for working. Apparently, we didn't listen though as both of us became cigarette smokers in high school. Light put off by the fire swirled around his face causing the chew to look like a round bump on one side.

Shorty said getting on to a scent could take Judy a while indicating we may as well get comfortable. Usually, at least three or four dogs hunted at one time to cover more ground. Comfortable wasn't a word I would have used. Maybe we could be somewhat less cold, but comfortable got left behind back at the house in my warm bed. More than once, while we waited, a deer, likely spooked by the hunting dog, rustled close by through the dry leaves. Each time the crashing sounded as though a full-grown mule had run through the woods. Shorty would shush us at the first hint of sound which grew louder as the deer got closer making its escape from the harmless dog. A coonhound would run a deer once in a while, but they could never catch one. Even Walker Hounds, bred to run deer, couldn't catch them unless they were injured. Grandpa Lewis said the hounds would run the deer clear out of the county. We never saw what made the noise crashing past us in the dark, but Shorty assured us they were nothing more than spooked deer.

Our fire began to feel good, but getting close enough to keep warm without getting burned presented a challenge. As usual, no matter where I sat the wind shifted blowing wood smoke into my eyes. It took no time at all for me to end up sitting in Shorty's lap. Warmth plus a feeling of safety, not to mention his invitation, made his lap a better option. It was much better than having my backside exposed to the woods where some creature other than a deer might run past or worse stop, grab, and carry me off into the cold night. Experience, of course, told me nothing worse than a bobcat lived in the bottom. Nobody ever got carried off, killed or eaten by a bobcat, but my imagination allowed for worse things out there in the darkness. Besides, cuddling close to him felt nice, though admitting it out loud would risk labeling me a sissy.

Almost an hour into the hunt, no sooner than our fire began to get comfortably warm, Shorty quieted us saying, "Listen, listen."

Junior and I shared a look but couldn't hear anything.

"That's Judy, I done heard some fine bayin over the years, but that there is music to my old ears," he said, "let's go boys. Let's put out this here fire."

We all stood. Shorty began kicking the sticks in the fire apart with his boot spreading them about. Before we had the fire out good Junior and I could hear Judy too. Mama had sent along leftovers from dinner wrapped in a towel which she tucked into a small bucket with a lid for us to snack on. She said it would help us keep warm to have something in our belly. We had eaten a good bit of it. Junior stuffed the leftovers into his breast coat pocket using the empty bucket to douse the fire with the freezing creek water. After a couple of minutes, no trace of the fire remained. We began moving together in the direction of Judy's raccoon song behind Shorty's lead.

Broken branches with downed sweet gum and cedar trees covered the ground, some rotting, others newly fallen making the going rough as we couldn't see good carrying nothing more than lanterns for light. An occasional blackberry thicket added to the difficulty as did the relentless icy wind. My brother and I tried to stay close behind Shorty who proceeded at a good clip smashing down briars or stepping around holes while showing us what to step over or what to step around. The dog's baying grew louder as we got closer. At last we could see Judy moving around the base of a lone hickory. She looked up occasionally trying to confirm the scent of whatever unfortunate raccoon her nose indicated had holed up there. The tree, or what remained, stood in a small clearing with no others nearby. The ground around the tree's base had downed limbs with several tree trunks strewn about. Judy's tree couldn't be more than a ten-foot tall stump of a hollow limbless hickory. With no other trees nearby, whatever animal climbed inside the hickory stump had virtually no escape route. Holding the lanterns high above our heads we looked hard for a raccoon. Something had dug a large hole into the rotting stump visible at the tree's base. Another hole at the top offered an alternative exit.

Junior looked over to Shorty saying, "That's the end of this coon hunt."

Experienced hunters had taught us a raccoon holed up would remain in the hole for safety. We expected Shorty to gather Judy up moving far enough away she wouldn't come back to this same dead-end. Hopefully we could interest her in going another direction.

But we were wrong.

The three of us stood there in the cold looking up and down the dead tree when Shorty handed me his lantern saying, "Hold this, it's okay boys, we'll jiss smoke him out."

Immediately, he began taking off his coat, shirt and finally his undershirt. Why would he be taking off his shirt? Junior and I were beyond freezing while Shorty stood there half-undressed. Before either of us could verbalize what we both wondered he began to shred the undershirt into long strips. With the shirt in shreds, stuffing the pieces into the hole at the bottom of the dead tree completed his plan.

'This is not happening.' I thought.

Breaking a fat dry stick from a downed pine tree limb he lifted the globe on one of the lanterns, lit the stick and placed the burning end under the torn pieces of shirt.

'My gosh. With the wind blowing like this we are gonna burn down the woods with us in them.' The entire scene had me wondering what to expect next.

As the fire grew larger inside the hole, thick grey smoke began escaping from the top, first a trickle before billowing like a wooden chimney. The dead tree, like a tall black candle, lit the woods with an eerie shadowy light. Shorty figured it right. Judy's raccoon could not stay inside with all the smoke and fire. Within less than a minute his head stuck out the hole at the top. The lanterns wouldn't cast light high enough for us to see well. Tree, smoke, and fire with a raccoon moving its head in and out of the hole, the trapped animal itself on fire, made for a surreal spectacle. My brother and I had never seen anything as unbelievable and never expected to again.

"Stand back, be ready, he's gonna jump any second." No sooner had Shorty blurted out the warning than his prediction proved accurate.

The raccoon leaped like a flying torch as far as possible. Upon hitting the ground it stood face to face with Judy, raccoon to dog. Junior and I were ready, ready to run should a mad, burning raccoon come at us like a torch with teeth. Junior wouldn't have much chance to get a safe shot off with all of us right there plus Judy only inches from the animal's teeth. Besides, with everything happening at a mind-boggling pace the gun wasn't even loaded yet. No game had presented itself until now. A fight ensued with the old dog trying to stay away from the raccoon's teeth on one end while avoiding the fire on the other end. It seemed as though a hundred acres of woods would catch on fire as the fight continued ten yards from the tree which was, by now, engulfed in flames, creating plenty of light for us to watch the animals fight. When the snarling, growling, hissing battle ended the coon lay dead with Judy continuing to bite and shake the half-burned carcass every bit as hard as Pepper would shake a bush. She must have had the taste of burnt coon bacon in her mouth.

After putting on his shirt and coat again Shorty tied a small rope around the dead animal's hind legs. Throwing the blackened carcass over his shoulder he said, "Well boys, let's go find us another one."

What remained of the tree began smoldering as the fire died down. Also, through a major miracle, or as a result of the damp forest floor, nothing else around us caught fire. Lucky for us the floor of the bottom woods was too wet to burn.

Junior and I stood stunned with mouths gaping. Neither of us had ever seen anything remotely similar to this coon hunt. Before we could get over the shock Shorty had taken his lantern back from me beginning to move away through the dark. Before we got a mere ten yards Judy began to vocalize she had caught another scent.

"Why would another raccoon be anywhere near such a noisy fight?" Junior asked no one in particular.

Raising our lanterns high we searched the forest floor in the direction of Judy's crashing through the undergrowth no more than ten or fifteen feet in front of us. The creek ran nearby. Although not wide at this spot it could be deep enough for a raccoon to drown a dog, a real concern on every hunt. Judy had reached the creek bank when she jumped on another raccoon. Once again the calm bottom woods filled with a growling brawl of fur, blood, and confusion. An unbelievably short fight resulted in a second dead raccoon.

But before anyone could say anything or move, Shorty blurted out, "That coon done slipped his rope and climbed right off my back. This old coon dog killed him again."

Shock became utter disbelief. My brother and I couldn't endure one more minute of the inconceivable event happening before our eyes. Had the cold numbed our senses to the point of hallucination? We never figured out how an animal as heavy as a full grown raccoon could wiggle its leg out of a rope, climbing off Shorty's back without him noticing. Maybe the cold numbed his ability to notice after standing shirtless throughout the melee earlier. Judy went on to find two more raccoons the same night but they treed high enough we couldn't see them or get a clean shot. We didn't get back home until the early morning hours.

Asleep before we got out of the woods, Shorty carried me most of the way home. My brother carried the raccoons with one tired old coon dog dragging along leading the way. Junior and I have been on other coon hunts over the years but nothing ever as memorable or exciting. Judy got sick again the next spring. This time Shorty couldn't do anything but try to keep her comfortable. She died in her sleep saving him the anguish of having to put her down. The three of us took her down to the bottom burying her next to the burned out hollow tree. Shorty said she would want to lay there near the raccoons. She had spent her life chasing them through the woods which made me wonder where they should bury me one day. Just about everybody gets buried in a cemetery close to relatives but my strong preference for dogs over people might suggest someplace different.

Shorty's Hard Story

Spring of 1936 came bringing warm weather earlier than normal. Another planting season had begun. Junior would turn fourteen in April and I had grown bigger. We helped Shorty a lot more than the years before. With an earlier start, plus cooperation from the weather, the three of us got the cotton planted by early April. One afternoon in May Grandpa Eddie came by. Shorty, Junior and I were working in the barn when the back screen door slammed which usually meant Wes coming out to begin his chores or Mama sending him to bring us something to eat. It was neither this time. Grandpa Eddie showed up at the barn door.

"Hello boys, hello Shorty," he said, his usual greeting.

My brother and I answered at the same time, "Hi Grandpa."

Shorty greeted him the same way he did all other white people with mister, saying, "Evenin Mister Eddie."

We continued our work mucking out Jane's stall to put fresh straw down. Grandpa walked over saying, "Looks like you boys found something you know how to do. Raking out Jane's dirty straw takes a lot of know how."

"Thanks for the compliment Grandpa," Junior's sarcasm fit perfectly with Grandpa's backhanded compliment.

"Shorty, one of the Harlow boys, Sam I believe, has been asking in town where you live. Those boys are never up to anything good. Why would he be asking around about you?" Grandpa asked.

Shorty, sitting on a stool replacing a broken lead on Jane's harness, looked up at him. Junior and I looked at each other, none of us saying anything.

From all the looks, Grandpa knew to pursue his question further. "Junior, you and Johnny go find something else to keep you busy for a while. I need to have a private conversation with Shorty."

Again, at first, none of us said anything causing Grandpa to continue, "Or is there something the three of you want to tell me?"

Having presented his challenge Grandpa stood with eyebrows raised, hands on his hips waiting like always when wanting to make us nervous.

It worked. Junior, the most forthright of anybody in our family, spoke first, "Mama told us we couldn't talk about it."

"Junior," I tried to stop him. "Don't say anything, even to Grandpa."

Grandpa shuffled his feet, took off his hat and gave me a stern look. After thinking on my comments he looked back at my brother saying, "That's fair enough. You boys are sayin I should talk to your mama then?"

He finished his question with another stare going between my brother and me. Without a doubt, his next move would be turning around to go back inside.

Shorty broke the silence, "Mister Eddie, I spect that Harlow boy might be mad at me."

"You didn't do nearly what he deserved," Junior blurted out, caught himself, and stood quietly.

After another minute of silent glances Grandpa said, "Junior, you and your brother let me have a few minutes alone with Shorty."

Neither of us wanted to make him angry. Never seeing him really mad, the idea of what an angry Grandpa Eddie might be like wasn't worth risking.

Handing the harness with a piece of new leather to Junior, Shorty said, "Take this into the house and see if'n you can finish up the stitching. I done showed you how so go on now. You go with him too Johnny. Let me talk to your grandpa here."

Both men said nothing more watching us until we were through the screen door into the kitchen. But making a beeline for the front door, I worked my way around to the back side of Jane's stall where everything the grownups said could be heard. Junior would never do anything so sneaky. He believed if Grandpa didn't want us to listen we should stay inside the house out of respect. For me, knowing what Grandpa and Shorty discussed far outweighed the relevance of some kind of unspoken respect. Listening didn't seem disrespectful if the result might help somehow. A crack in the siding allowed me to listen while watching everything going on in the barn. They were already talking.

Grandpa said, "I know it's not like you to make trouble especially with whites. And I respect the fact Emilie told the boys not to say anything, but this thing sounds like something involving them too. All I want to do is help if I can. What's goin on Shorty?"

"Mister Eddie, I appreciate you bein concerned. I don't want to cause no trouble to Miss Emilie and these fine chillrens of hers. She tolt the boys not to say nothin to protect me I spect. But if'n you was to do somethin about all this, trouble might come for them. I sure don't want that, no siree."

Grandpa looked around, picked up the feed bucket, placed it on the ground upside down across from Shorty, and sat. An oft-used strategy of his during a serious discussion had long been to take his time, being deliberate before saying anything.

Holding his hat with both hands close to the ground between his legs, he began again, "I don't know if I can promise I won't do anything. It's not like me to let things go if they aren't right. But I can promise I'll help any way I can. Leaving something between people unresolved, especially something involving those boys is the wrong thing to do."

"I agrees with you sir, I would have come to you before except Miss Emilie asked us all not to say no more bout it. You see, this all puts me in a hard place."

"I understand what you're saying. But you gotta trust I'll do right by you on this Shorty. You believe I will try, don't you?"

"Yes sir, I believe you will."

"You all got me worried if it's something Em wants to keep quiet. How did all of them get involved?"

Shorty went right to the heart of it. "Well sir, it's about Miss Sara."

"Sara?" Grandpa Eddie knew right away something involving Sam Harlow and Sara wasn't good.

"Yes sir, but she's okay. He didn't hurt her none, but he come in tryin to bother her here at the house one day last November right around Thanksgiving if I remember right."

Grandpa raised his head with eyes wide open maybe to hear more clearly.

"He didn't hurt her or nothin. I wouldn't let nothin like that happen." Shorty added.

Grandpa cut him off, "Back up now, start over. You mean Sam, right? I want to hear all of it, every single thing."

"Yes sir, it was Mister Sam. Miss Emilie took the boys down to Pearson's to buy them each a pair of new shoes, but Miss Sara didn't go along. She walked herself home from school. I had come out here to the hog pen workin on the fence where the big sow busted out when I heard a fuss there in the house. Next thing I know Miss Sara shouted Mister Sam's name, telling him to leave her alone. None of what she said sounded good. I didn't remember him bein one of them Harlow boys til I went in and there he stood."

"What happened?"

Watching his expressions while listening through the crack, Grandpa's tone became more serious than ever. He sat now flipping his mustache thinking while he listened. The idea of getting caught began to worry me.

"Well I jiss run in the kitchen, grabbin up that ole eight-gauge of Mister William's. When I come into the living room there they stood by the front door, Miss Sara tryin to get out I suppose with him holdin on to her. She tried pushin him away. I could see she been cryin. That got me plenty mad Mister Eddie. There weren't no time to get shells, if'n I couldn't bluff him with the empty gun I'd use the barrel on him. I pointed the gun right at him and told him to git on away from here. It didn't take him much thinkin before he let go of her. She come over by me. While goin out the door he shouted out some kind of threat or other. I didn't pay it no mind. I've had plenty of threats from peoples like him before. I held onto Miss Sara for a while til her mama and the boys come home. Miss Emilie talked things over with the chillren deciding not to tell anybody. She did so to protect me I spect. There weren't no reason for her to do that Mister Eddie."

He paused while Grandpa assessed the situation before saying, "She had every reason to protect you. You're as much family as anyone. I'm sure Em realized no one would listen to her side of the story. There are enough bad folks out there who would use any excuse to come after you for threatening a white. Em knew Sam would have a different version and probably already told his daddy and brother just in case she decided to make a stink about it. I'll talk to Em to let her know what you told me. I agree with her on keeping this quiet, but you keep an eye out. Sam Harlow is up to no good going around asking about you."

"I ain't afraid of those peoples. Pepper will let me know if anybody comes around my place. I keeps my pistol with me all the time when I'm not in my cabin. I ain't gonna get myself caught up gettin kilt like my pappy did."

He caught himself. Stopping he looked at his shoes. Grandpa could have let the conversation end right there, but he rarely let go of anything serious.

"What happened to your pappy?"

"I don't need to bother you none with all that Mister Eddie. It all happened a long time ago."

But while finishing his response his eyes reddened either from anger or sadness. Having seen Shorty's eyes well up Grandpa would press him to say more. He always tried to convince me to talk about hard things, things difficult to bring up to an adult. Shorty had little chance of avoiding more discussion.

Grandpa repeated himself adding, "You can tell me what happened. I want to know because I care."

Shorty began, "He got kilt when I was near bout ten years ole. We lived down around Senatobia. My pappy and mammy made they livin as tenmant, I mean tenant farmers, on property owned by the son of Charles Benton. Old man Benton was the last of the Bentons to own the Benton plantation takin up near bout the whole county kindof like the boys other grandpa, Mister Lewis' place. Pappy and Mammy worked real hard. They never did cause nobody any trouble, barely making enough money to pay off Mr. Benton for the supplies he bought for them during the year. Every year they would start over again. Even when my folks had a good year with the cotton the owner always came up with some reason why they didn't make any money. They talked about their money problems secretly but didn't know us kids could hear em. My pappy knew Mr. Benton jiss took advantage of them every year making hisself rich off them and the others like them, but there weren't nothin they could do. Lots of other folks jiss got up and lef for Chicago or places where real jobs were, but my folks wanted to stay in Mississippi, they home. They never went to school, but they weren't dumb people."

Grandpa cut in, "I'm sure they weren't dumb. Plenty of tenant farming still goes on today. Neither white nor black folks can make a living at it. What happened to your pappy?"

It became obvious Shorty would have a hard time telling the next part as he gathered himself and exhaled before continuing, "Well sir, I had a brother. Mammy named him Ezekiel. He had just turned fifteen when it all happened. Pappy sent him into town one day to fetch a new straw hat for Mammy to wear in the fields. My pappy worked hard to save a little bit of money for her birthday. He told Zeke to go along careful as usual about doing anything that could get him in trouble. Zeke was smart though. He had been to town by himself many times since turning twelve. But this day went different. Plenty of time had gone by for him to run the errand but still he didn't come back. Pappy had to tell Mammy a small lie about why Zeke went to town or else spoil her surprise."

"Near bout sundown, Zeke's friend from another farm came running up to the house all out of breath scared like nothin I had ever seen before. Pappy and Mammy sat on the front porch. The boy calmed down enough to tell Pappy how Zeke got himself caught up by a bunch of bad white folks. They claimed he looked at a white girl scaring her. She said he bumped into her in the store in a bad way sayin it wasn't no accident. Zeke's friend said a bunch of whites had gathered talking bout hangin him. My pappy had tolt us kids over and over bout this kind of thing, how a black man could get hung or burned alive for most anything if they got crossways with a bad white person. Pappy knew the Sheriff would never do anything more than pretend to look out for justice."

"Pappy tolt Mammy to keep us chillren inside cause he had to go into town to see what he could do. Mammy got worried and started cryin pleading with him to go to the Sheriff. Pappy told her he would be careful, but he had to go help his boy. I spect that's why Mammy got upset. She knew Pappy would put his own self in danger to help any of us. No sooner had he left down the road than I told

Mammy I was going too. She could have held me, but she couldn't catch me. I stayed back a safe distance, knowing a ten-year-old black boy couldn't do nothin more than watch against all those white folks."

"Pappy would have sent me back anyhow if he saw me followin' along. When I got into the edge of town I saw near bout fifty white peoples. They had my brother and my pappy tied up standing side by side. The white folks shouted all kinds of bad words, ugly things. Some of them people aimed their words at the Sheriff who stood back a little from the crowd. He wore his gun but never hinted at taking it out of the holster. Finally, two big fellows carryin pistols pushed the Sheriff away from the crowd. I guess he knew better than to try any further."

"Still plenty of shoutin continued when somebody come up in a empty horse drawn wagon. They tied Pappy and Zeke to the back. The wagon driver whipped and hollered at his horses. Down the main street they went. Pappy and Zeke fell right away, gettin dragged along. The crowd ran behind on foot yellin while tryin to follow along as best they could. I got feelin sick thinkin I might throw up. I couldn't help, alls I could think of was my mammy. There in the street all trampled on, torn up, lay her new birthday hat. I cried so hard I couldn't see too good but began to follow along." Shorty stopped again staring at the ground.

Grandpa said, “If you can’t say anything more it’s okay.”

“No sir, it’s fine, I never tolt anybody after all these years. I needs to get it out of me. I followed behind the crowd of angry people down a side road out into the country more than a mile. They dragged Pappy and Zeke the entire way. When they stopped those men lifted em all bloodied into the back of the wagon. After throwing ropes over a tree limb they pulled the wagon away and hung em both. All that draggin should’ve kilt em but didn’t. Fallin out the back of the wagon with a rope on their necks wasn’t enough to kill em neither. Mister Eddie they jerked and coughed, choking while those men yelled terrible things. Before they died others came up with torches lighting their clothes on fire. It was all like the worst dream ever. In jiss no time my brother and Pappy got caught up, dragged, hung and burnt alive. The next day somebody said they saw the bodies of two Negroes in the back of a wagon burnt crispy. They said the bodies had burnt crispy Mister Eddie like they was nothin more than a piece of meat.”

With that, he paused again.

After a short while, Grandpa said, “There’s nothing I can say to make any difference. I’ve heard about those kinds of lynching’s my whole life but fortunately, have never seen any of them happen. There’s not a more vile way humans can treat other humans. I almost don't feel I have the right to ask for your forgiveness as a white man. I've tried to make sure my actions always show there's a better way. How people can treat others with such awful hate makes my soul ache. Hating people for no reason other than their differences is not right. God says it's wrong but it's also ignorant. The results are always disgusting...."

Shorty stopped Grandpa, "I knows yer heart's good sir. I sees it in Miss Emilie, too, and I sees the same goodness in her chillren. You're not responsible for somethin another man does that's wrong. Alls we can do as men is be responsible for our ownself and try to teach our chillren the right way. Coming to it took me a lot of years. I stored up a lot of hate for too many years before decidin hatin wasn't gonna bring my pappy and brother back. Neither was it gonna make bad whites quit bein bad. I've seen more good whites than bad ones, truth be tolt. But none of them things mean I'm gonna stand back letting the likes of Sam Harlow do harm to me or any of this here Cook family. I'll die first but I won't be the onliest one dyin."

Nothing Shorty ever said before sounded as emphatic. His face had gone from dark brown to red from anger. Gentler than a cool breeze on a hot day all the years I knew him his one statement to Grandpa in the barn told me so much more. The gentle man had a toughness, a sense of fairness, and an inner strength I recognized but didn't fully understand at the time.

Grandpa placed a hand on Shorty's shoulder saying nothing at first. Removing his hand he extended an open palm saying, "I'm quite privileged and proud to know you, Mr. Ashford. I hope you can call me a friend."

I had forgotten Shorty's real name but Grandpa hadn't. As usual, Shorty seemed ill at ease, at first, about shaking with a white person, but soon he reached across taking Grandpa's hand, the two shaking heartily.

"We need to go talk to Em and the kids. We'll do whatever we can to keep this Harlow business from getting out of hand."

"Thank you sir; and thank you for bein my friend," Shorty said.

Tears ran down my face. Mesmerized by the conversation, I forgot to move from my hiding place before Grandpa came out of the barn.

He would see me trying to sneak away for sure which didn't matter as he said, "Johnny come out from behind there, let's go in the house."

How did he know? But the tone of his voice didn't suggest I would be in trouble. Around the corner of the barn, Grandpa stood smiling with Shorty standing by his side.

Putting his arm around my shoulder as we walked toward the house together he leaned over,

"Life is a lot harder for some folks than for others. All we can do is try to make sure we ain't the ones making it hard for others. Are you okay Johnny?"

"Yes sir, I'll be okay."

Looking over at Shorty, his face ashen and somber, I took his hand garnering a half-smile from him as the three of us proceeded into the house. Grandpa explained to Mama all he had heard about Sara asking Sara if she was okay now. Again as before everyone agreed nothing else would be said unless the Harlow's made more trouble. Grandpa said nothing to anyone about Shorty's hard story. I never told anybody else, including my older brother.

My grandpa and Shorty had taught me more about people in a matter of minutes than I have learned the rest of my life. They taught me real life, not fiction or hearsay or somebody's version of politics, positioning or power. Shorty's hard story had told a truth of how horrible people can act with respect to others with no justification while Grandpa's actions toward him showed a kindness crossing over the boundaries of color. Not difficult to understand or complicated in the least, the matter seemed simple yet unfair to a degree impossible to describe. But experience has proven again and again in my life how all of us so often get it wrong to varying degrees.

Trouble in the Dark

Not long afterward, Junior came home from town telling Mama some of his friends heard Sam and Teddy Harlow had found out where Shorty lived. They said they were coming after him sometime at night. The news didn't come directly from the Harlow's but any kind of threat spread pretty quickly. Regardless if Sheriff Barton confirmed the rumor he couldn't do much. Talking to the Harlow's or their daddy wouldn't accomplish anything. Their daddy would tell him to mind his own business, as though threats against people were not his business. Anyhow, white people didn't pay any attention to threats against black people. They were such a regular occurrence nobody paid attention or cared. Mama told me to find Shorty. She warned him to stay on his guard telling him she would have Junior ride Jane to Grandpa Lewis' for help if anyone ever came around making trouble. Of course, Shorty in return told her not to worry. He did not want Junior or any of us to get involved with any trouble on his account.

Many nights later lying awake in bed listening for trouble, I tried to figure out what might happen expecting to hear a crowd of people out of control coming with a wagon for Shorty. Obviously, no one would come with a wagon since it was 1936. It wasn't 1890, but the idea of a wagon stuck in my head from the story Shorty told Grandpa. Thinking about all the horrible things they might do made falling asleep plenty difficult reminding me of many sleepless nights after first hearing Shorty's story. Lynching had become rare by the late 1930s, but stories circulated too often of a dead black person hauled through some small town, tied to the front of a pickup like a deer, or found in the edge of a cotton field along a dirt road. Of course, no one ever had any idea how the people died. The authorities never seemed to try finding out what happened beyond some initial questioning of the person dropping off or finding a body. Even as a white person the mysterious deaths produced an inexplicable darkness, an evil existing around us.

On two occasions Junior mentioned in front of Shorty something he heard about an unsolved death of a black person. My brother had no idea the real reason Shorty would never engage in a conversation about the incidents beyond the obvious fact he was a black man. I would simply look at Junior shaking my head, no, saying nothing.

The second time it happened he asked me later, in private, "Hey, I guess it's a mistake bringing up news in front of Shorty about those black people getting killed with no one knowing how. I just thought he would want to know, but you seem almost as reluctant as he is. Is there something more I don't know?"

He had put me on the spot. If Shorty hadn't told him there was a reason, it wasn't for me to say. "It's got to be harder for him to talk about than us. I just don't bring up those kinds of things around him."

Skirting the real issue without telling a complete lie apparently worked. He went to Shorty and apologized. Apology accepted, Shorty simply told him there wasn't any need to dwell on something he couldn't do anything about. He said he just wished all those troubles between people would end some day. Junior felt bad. He never again mentioned the subject around Shorty.

The Harlows would have to come right past our house on the way to Shorty's cabin which gave me plenty of time to wake up Mama and Junior. But knowing Shorty had Pepper there to warn him put my mind a little more at ease. Tossing about each night struggling to doze off, before long our rooster would be crowing outside the next morning waking up everybody in the house, including every animal we had.

More than a week passed since Junior's report about the Harlow's. Though often playing jokes on us this wasn't something even my brother would make a game out of. More days went by. On a hot Saturday, we had spent all day working the cotton. The work week had been long. Our family began getting ready for bed, we were all tired. Shorty had gone to his cabin after dinner. Lying on top of the bed covers with a full stomach seemed the best way to end the day. Mama and Sara were still in the kitchen evident by the light filtering underneath the bedroom door. Not long after Mama put out the lanterns we heard gunshots, first one, then another, then silence. At first, we couldn't tell for sure if the noise was gunfire. Without question though the sound came from down the hill where Shorty lived. We listened another couple of minutes. A third shot came, followed by a fourth.

"Junior, you hear that?" I said.

He already had his feet on the floor pulling his overalls on, reaching for his boots, "Yeah, I gotta go, you go for Grandpa Lewis."

Before Junior and I could get out of bed Mama had a lantern lit coming into our room. "Junior, get the harness on Jane and ride for Grandpa's. Shorty may be in trouble."

Junior had other plans though.

"Someone's shootin at him. There ain't no time to get help. I'm takin the eight-gauge to help him. I can slip to the edge of the woods by his cabin. Whoever is there will never hear or see me. When they shoot again I can see where they are by the flash of their guns. If I hit em with number six-shot from the eight-gauge they won't stay around to find out who's shootin."

Mama started to protest, but he cut her off, "I gotta go Mama."

He made his case more adamant than ever. She gave in.

"You be careful. Promise me you'll stay back in the trees. I'll send Johnny to your grandpa's."

"I promise Mama, I'll be okay," Junior answered as he went through the back door.

Being a good shot Junior would have no problem scaring them away. Mama standing at the screen door watching Junior go across the backyard gave me the chance to slip over and get the other shotgun. Before she could turn around I went out the front door. She called for me to come back until I got behind the barn catching up with my brother.

"You're gonna get yourself killed and Mama is gonna kill you if you don't," he said.

He may have been right, but one way or the other no one could stop me from helping my friend. "I'm goin too. I'll go without you if I have to."

We had no time to argue. Junior knew I had become a pretty good shot too. He agreed right away, "All right but you keep your head down. If you get killed Mama will kill me for sure." Before finishing he added with a smile, "Be careful Bud."

We didn't take a lantern. Someone could see us approaching with any kind of light. Anyhow, we knew the woods to Shorty's place like the back of our hand. We had tromped down a well-worn path over many trips. Either of us could have made the short trek with our eyes closed. But with the cloudy sky making everything around us pitch black, we were running blind. Going as fast as we could, we got within about fifty yards when two then three more shots came from Shorty's place.

Junior turned saying quietly, "We gotta move like we are deer hunting, putting one foot in front of the other so quiet breaking a twig won't make a sound. But we gotta move quicker than deer hunting. You work your way around to the northwest corner of the cabin. Get the big oak between you and anyone who could be on the front porch. I'll go straight through the woods to the front. The shooting sounds like it's coming from there. Get going but, hey, be careful not to shoot me or Shorty by mistake. As a matter of fact, try not to shoot at all unless you have to."

Junior tried to convince me the plan wouldn't be too dangerous for him with me covering him while he worked his way around from the side. After my brother moved off it took a few seconds for me to get my wits about me wondering what getting shot would be like. Junior must have had me go around to the back to keep me out of danger while he went straight into it, a lot for this eleven-year-old to think about. Choosing a target in the dark had me more than a little concerned. The possibility of shooting him or Shorty scared me worse than getting shot myself.

Meanwhile, Pepper's non-stop barking continued though no other sounds came from inside Shorty's house. Moving to a spot where light inside the cabin could be seen took an unbelievable number of careful steps. More than once my foot came down on a dry twig. I had learned what twigs and larger branches felt like under my shoe in time to either back off or continue putting pressure downward carefully enough the snap would make an insignificant amount of noise. A methodical enough step would sometimes not break the stick at all. The challenge of making no sound when stepping on one had become a game. But this was no game to sneak up on a deer in its bed. Successfully navigating through the dark could determine whether Shorty lived through the night, or my brother or even me.

But once there, two torches came into view, glowing brightly on the edge of the woods in the front. Whoever held the torches stood about three or four yards apart concealed by the trees. Shorty's well sat between the oak tree and the cabin. Out in the open, it offered less protection but a good place to watch for Junior. The well gave me enough cover to sneak out low to the ground. Squatting, I waited next to the rock base built three feet above the ground forming a circle. From my vantage point, the corner of the front porch wasn't visible though. Neither was Junior moving through the woods. By now he should have seen the torches. Hopefully, he wouldn't come out into the open in front of the cabin until doing so would not result in being shot.

Probably close to a hundred years old, the cabin had been literally built from pine tree logs most likely cut in close enough proximity to minimize hauling them a long distance. The resulting yard area was clear within thirty yards of the tiny house on all sides. Anyone trying to approach unwanted would have a dangerous open area to cross. Doing so after dark, however, would be relatively easy.

Pepper's constant barking made hearing anything coming from inside the cabin impossible. The thought of finding Shorty dead and having to go through life without him began to worry me. Everything moved at a snail's pace. Occasionally someone fired shots at the cabin, coming from the direction the torches were in. The muzzle flash of each shot lit up the darkness for an instant as much as the booming obliterated the quiet. My mind wandered, 'What made this happen, why did bad things follow good people like Shorty their entire life.' Sometimes Pepper stopped barking. The scene became dead quiet except for the people mumbling close to the torches.

Someone yelled out. It was one of the Harlows, "We know you're in there Negro. You come on out here and meet us like a man if you are one or we'll torch your shanty shack with you in it."

Still no response from the cabin other than Pepper's barking. My mouth wanted to call out to Shorty, telling him my brother and I were outside to help, but my head took control for once, besides, Junior had told me to keep quiet.

The same voice called out again, "Old man, this is your last warning. We'll burn you up in there. I'm gonna count to three...."

Apparently, the Harlows were trying to bluff Shorty to come out. Setting the old cabin on fire would not be an easy task. The tin roof wouldn't catch fire. Setting fire to the outside would require a long accurate toss of a torch or else crossing the open area to throw it through a window. The first option wasn't good. The second option might get someone shot.

The counting never reached three. The eight-gauge went off, both barrels, one right after the other. The shotgun blast created a lot of yelling. One torch dropped to the ground. Within no time the eight-gauge went off again, both barrels. This produced more screaming with quite a commotion of people running through the woods making more racket than a herd of scared deer. One torch lay burning on the ground while the other one could be seen bouncing through the trees as the two culprits made their way to the main road. Everything else around the cabin became still and silent. After a minute or so the noise created by whoever ran off faded away. Still, though, I stayed down behind the well for a long time listening. Everything around the entire area remained quiet; including the dog. Junior appeared at the edge of the woods, walking in the shadows made by the light from the dropped torch. He was an easy target if the danger had not already gone, running up the hill.

"Shorty, it's Junior and Johnny. We're outside. Those troublemakers ran off through the woods. Are you okay?" Junior called out.

Standing and moving around to the side, I stepped back into the cover of the trees, giving me a better view of the front porch. We waited with no answer for another minute or two when the front door opened. A giant, unearthly shadow projected inside the cabin created by a profile of Shorty holding his pistol in one hand with a lantern and Pepper tugging at his leash in the other. The man looked bigger than ever to me. Light flickered all about him, partly as a breeze blew across the lantern's wick through the newly opened door, but more so from the terrier jerking against the leash.

There haven't been many times in my life when seeing someone made me happier.

Holding the lantern high to look out into the darkness off the front edge of the porch he stood for a moment before saying, "Junior is that you?"

"Yeah, it's me. Johnny is here too."

"Why, what is you boys doin over here gettin all tangled up in Shorty's mess? Get yerselves in here before whoever was out there decides to come back around."

We ran jumping on the small porch, neither of us touching the rock used for a step. Shorty let go of Pepper nearly losing his grip on the lantern as my brother and I slammed in to him. With a big arm around each of us, he began to admonish us again doing his best to act serious while continuing to search blindly out across the front yard.

"Now boys, yer mama is gonna be worried outta her head. What made you do a fool thing like comin down here with all this shootin goin on?"

Convincing us we did not need to come to his aid seemed more an act than anything.

Junior said, "Mama wanted us to go to Grandpa Lewis' for help but we thought it would take too long. We were afraid for you."

The old man could no longer pretend he was upset asking, "Did you fire off that ole shotgun Junior? From the sounds of those rascals after you bore down on em I believe you musta busted em good. Yes sir you busted em real good."

Shorty's compliment made Junior quite proud of himself. My brother's smile and excited response left no question about it. "Yes sir, I could see em pretty clear standing in the torchlight, Sam and Teddy Harlow. Sam did all the talking. They got a big enough mouth on em but I'm pretty sure I got em both good. I shot low so as not to hurt em too bad, but I've seen enough rabbits shot with number sixes. Those pellets will tear under their skin all the way through their overalls."

The three of us with Pepper's help did quite a bit of looking around out where the torch lay smoldering, burned out. Broken sticks laid about with the dirt kicked up, signs of somebody making a hasty exit. Blood splatters were here and there in the dirt. There was also blood on sticks lying around where each of them had been standing. Tracks led back up the hill toward the highway.

Mama had sent Sara to Grandpa Lewis' but by the time Uncle Wes and Grandpa came in the pickup, we were sitting on the porch. Grandpa said going after the Harlows at night might not be safe. After telling him who they were and why they had come around he sent Uncle Wes to bring back Sheriff Barton. Grandpa stayed with us, a twelve-gauge in hand with his six shot long barrel .44 pistol in a holster on his hip. He said the Harlow's wouldn't get too far away if they took on a bunch of lead pellets from Daddy's eight-gauge.

Grandpa Lewis was right. The Harlow brothers showed up at Doctor Jones' later the same night claiming they were cleaning a shotgun when the gun accidentally went off shooting one of them in the back of the legs and the other in the butt. When questioned the next day by the Sheriff neither of them could explain how they got shot from behind while cleaning a gun. And they couldn't explain how their accident happened the same night someone got scared away from the cabin of Emilie Cook's farm hand. They never did find out who shot them. Later on, the Sheriff questioned them in separate rooms. After speaking to each individually he got different stories. They weren't smart enough to realize they should agree on one story and keep it straight. The Sheriff threw them in jail to go before the judge the next week.

After realizing prison appeared imminent for them both, Teddy broke down blaming everything on his brother for bothering the Cook girl back in the fall. His brother accusing him didn't sit well with Sam precipitating a fist fight between the brothers in the Sheriff's office. Sheriff Barton had to hold them in separate cells. The juries in those days were all-white. But this particular jury had no difficulty convicting white men for doing something against a black man. The overwhelming evidence included the incident between Sam Harlow and Sara which put a nail in it for him. Both Harlows were found guilty of trespassing and attempted murder. The judge sent them both to the state prison at Parchment Farm. The adults always said you never want to end up at the Parchment Prison Farm. The Harlow brothers were not going to bother anybody around the Cook place, or any place else, for a long time.

Sara Goes to College

During the next two years, things didn't get any better around the country. Millions of people were still out of work as the Depression entered its ninth year, 1938. Wes was eleven and helping out more with the farming. My thirteenth birthday was in May and Junior turned sixteen the month before. The end of May Sara graduated from high school with honors. She, with one other boy from Holly Springs High School, was selected for the National Honor Society. Junior said only the smartest people got in the Honor Society. He said for me not to spend a great amount of time thinking about it. Luckily, he went on to say both of us were smart enough which had nothing to do with why neither of us would get in.

He said, "You're plenty smart. You can be too smart for your own good sometimes. But people who get in the Honor Society are smart plus they work hard in school. Playing on the basketball team and skipping out for fishing or hunting season all the time isn't considered hard work which I'm sure explains why our grades aren't anything to brag about."

His logic wouldn't get any argument from me. Without question, we had different priorities from our big sister. She had actually become easier to live with too because when she punched me now I most likely deserved it. In the past the constant blaming and hitting had no point coming from nothing but meanness. Before graduation, Sara asked Grandpa Eddie to drive her and Mama over to Blue Mountain College in Tupelo to find out if she could get accepted there. She wanted to study Education. A girl's college in Tupelo, Blue Mountain College was about sixty miles from our farm.

Sara said she thought the school would not be too far from home, making it easy to come home on holidays or breaks, catching rides with other students on their way home to Memphis or riding the bus to Holly Springs. Though her high school accomplishments got her accepted she discovered no scholarships were available for the upcoming year. Without a scholarship to cover the $125 annual tuition and $300 fee for the dormitory and food going to college for her was out of the question. Our entire cotton crop in those days didn't bring in much more income than her college fees would have been.

Sara came back pretty depressed about her chances resigned to a life on the farm like all the other girls she knew. She did a good job of not taking it out on the rest of us though. At the end of June, a letter of congratulations came from the College. She had been accepted for admission. The college was thanking her for payment in full covering the first year's tuition, room and board. The letter came from the Dean. Including her, twenty-five young women were accepted from Mississippi along with a few from the surrounding states.

Excited but skeptical she said to Mama, "This can't be right. They must've meant to send this to someone else. Grandpa Eddie offered to help out but couldn't cover even the tuition. Grandpa Lewis didn't offer anything. He doesn't think anybody needs to go to college, especially a girl. I'm gonna write the school a letter to find out what's going on."

"No, you go over to your Grandpa and Grandma Daniel's. Use their telephone. There's a phone number right here at the bottom of your letter." Mama insisted.

Sara wasted no time. She rode Jane over to our grandparent's house. Leaving late in the afternoon she told Mama she would spend the night there returning the next morning. Around noon the next day she came home going into the kitchen to find Mama already working on dinner. On my way out the back door I heard her begin to tell what she learned.

After explaining her reason for calling, the Dean's secretary told her to wait while she pulled the file.

Returning in a few seconds the woman said, "Okay Miss Cook, I have a carbon copy of the letter you received from the Dean right in front of me. I remember typing it too because I was so excited. These situations are so rare it sends shivers all over me when I get to type one of these. To tell the truth I haven't typed one in a long time with the Depression and all. You know, I think Dean Davis was just as excited when he dictated it to me."

"Excuse me, but what situations Ma'am." Sara couldn't stand the suspense. The secretary's enthusiasm was nice but the anticipation it created for Sara was killing her.

"Well, it's not often one of our students offers to pay in full these days. There's a receipt for the deposit in the file with a banknote promising to pay the balance for your first year by the end of August. Are you saying you are not aware of this?"

"Yes ma'am, I mean no ma'am I'm not aware at all."

Sara said the secretary spoke again after a brief silence, "Well, I'm not surprised. My, what a wonderful surprise. Don't you think so Miss Cook?"

"Well, yes Ma'am, I guess so, I mean yes. But I still don't understand. Who would do such a thing for me?"

"Well, that certainly explains why the person making the payment asked us to keep his part confidential. He didn't use, didn't know, the word confidential, he just wanted his privacy. I went into the Dean's office with him for the meeting. We obviously realized what he meant by private. We told him we would be glad to protect his privacy. Of course, I'm sorry I can't tell you who the person was. All I can do is confirm your letter is accurate. Isn't it exciting? I will say I have never in all my years here had a white girl's tuition paid by a black man. Oh my, I may have said too much."

The secretary had leaked more than she dared about Sara's benefactor. She continued, "But I can say we were a little surprised to confirm with a banker the person offering to make payment has more than enough in an account to cover the balance. Otherwise, I'm sure Dean Davis would not have accepted the deposit. Is there anything else I can help you with Miss Cook?"

Sara said she sat there, too stunned to respond. The secretary repeated, "Miss Cook is there anything else?"

"No ma'am, uh, thank you ma'am."

After hanging up, Sara said she asked Grandpa and Grandma Daniels if they knew anything about the mystery. Unbeknownst to her, as well as everybody else, Grandpa Eddie knew but wasn't telling. He, too, had been sworn to secrecy plus he wanted her to figure the mystery out herself.

There was only one black fellow Sara knew well enough to do something like this, but the person she suspected was poor as a church mouse. He never bought anything new. His clothes, though always tattered and worn, were kept clean. His boots were probably newer but looked like the same ones from the day she first saw him at the cemetery. She told Mama she had to ask him anyhow. She didn't know where else to go for answers. Mama didn't know about the transaction either. Not wanting to miss what happened next I followed her out the back door.

As usual, Shorty had been long at work in the barn repairing Jane's stall, always finding something to work on. Sara going to the barn in the middle of the day was unusual. Seeing her coming, he intentionally kept his head down trying to avoid eye contact.

Stopping close in front of him she said, "Shorty."

He didn't look up.

"Shorty!"

This time his answer came with a poorly disguised act of surprise, "Oh, ah, good mornin to you Miss Sara. I didn't see you standin there."

She either didn't catch his act or else played along, "Shorty, I got accepted to Blue Mountain College, isn't that wonderful?"

"Yes um, I's real happy for you. That's what you wanted ain't it honey?"

"Of course it is. You know it is. Is there anything you need to tell me?"

He looked at her full in the face with raised eyebrows; his large brown eyes opened wide, "Uh, no ma'am. I don't have nothin to say exceptin I'm glad for you gettin in that girls school. You is gonna be mighty smart Miss Sara."

Getting nowhere with the subtle approach, she made a slight change. "The secretary at the college said somebody offered to pay for my tuition and dormitory fees. I don't know anybody with that kind of money."

"Well, honey, that's mighty nice. You sure deserve that kind of thing."

Sara stood now giving him the silent treatment probably picked up from Grandpa Eddie's style. After a few seconds, it began to work.

Shorty said, "I don't know nothin bout no down payment or dorma...dormitory, and I don't expect too many peoples got much money these days. This is sure mighty strange, mighty strange."

He went on with his work, head down.

Junior jumped in, "Sara, what in the name of Pete are you talking about and why are you asking Shorty?"

She decided to play along until she got the truth of the story right from his mouth. To Junior's face but for Shorty's ears she said, "Well, if you must know, apparently someone offered to pay for my college. The secretary at the college said a black man came in to set up the payments. Do you know any black men with that much money? Do you Johnny?"

Wes answered for both of us, "We don't know any white men with that kind of money."

Wes' comment earned a chuckle from Shorty.

Sara had planned to play the frustrated sister which she did with a high degree of success any time the need arose.

"What's so funny? I want to know what's going on. Am I the only person who doesn't know?" Her volume had increased slightly. But before anyone could speak she realized how Shorty had answered her. "I didn't say anything about a down payment being made."

Finally, looking her in the face her benefactor said, "No ma'am, I suppose you didn't. You ain't the onliest person who don't know neither honey. But one person who does is your grandpa, Mister Eddie."

Shorty had revealed enough for her to end the act.

Sara asked, “Did you go over to the college offering to pay my tuition and if you did how can you do that?”

He smiled, “Yes um, I am the guilty party I spect. I made a trip over there. That sure is some kind of fine school for you Miss Sara. They is real particular bout makin sure peoples can pay if'n they say they are gonna. Yes um, they made a phone call to the bank and talked to Mr. Gurley hisself while I sat right there waiting in the man's fine office with all them fine hardwood desks and chairs and carpets on the floor.”

Sara said, “What do you mean they called Mr. Gurley. You mean Mr. Gurley at the Bank of Holly Springs?”

“Yes ma'am Mr. Gurley hisself.”

Sara's patience had run out. Now she wanted the whole story, “Shorty, please tell me what's going on.”

His look softened, “Well, I hear'd how disappointed you been bout not bein able to go to college so I went over there to see if'n I could help any. You is plenty smart and all I kept hearin bout was the money part didn't work out. I went to ask Mister Eddie for his advice. He tolt me to go down to the bank to ask Mr. Gurley if'n he knew what I could do to help. Your grandpa tolt me Mr. Gurley went to one of them fine colleges hisself. Mr. Gurley, he done tolt me to go visit somebody called the Dean who I guess is the boss man at the college. I went over there two or three weeks back. They are right nice peoples at that college. They tolt me I jiss had to pay part of the total amount, the down payment. They said I could pay the rest later on after you decided for sure bout goin there. That's exactly what Mr. Gurley tolt me they would say. Course they called the bank first to make sure I had enough money. They had me sign a paper promisin to pay the rest when the note come due. They called the paper I signed some kind of Promise Note or something."

Sara could hardly speak. Through tears, she asked, "But how are you going to get the rest of the money?"

"Oh, I got the money already. There's a fair amount more too, I spect. I made my money workin on the railroad. Mister Eddie tolt me a long time ago I should put my money in the bank. He took me over to meet the man who run it before Mr. Gurley. I spect that's one of the onliest banks in the state that didn't lose everybody's money when the Depression come. Yes ma'am, I'm one lucky ole man to have all that money, but I never had nothin to spend none on til now. I asked Mr. Gurley several times over the years if'n I should use some to help out Miss Emilie and you chillren, but he said we all looked like we were stayin healthy enough. He said I should hold on until I needed it real bad for something. He is one smart man, Mr. Gurley. Mister Eddie, he didn't know I still had all my railroad money. Truth be tolt, after a while I forgot myself. Mr. Gurley said I earned me lots of interest on my money in all those years. They's plenty more left in the bank. Don't you worry none bout that."

Sara composed herself before asking, "But, why did you do it?"

"Awe, I knew all along goin to college meant more than anything to you. I didn't like you bein disappointed. You mean a lot more to ole Shorty than any amount of money sittin someplace collectin dust in a bank. And yer mama has done fed me more over these years than all my money could ever pay for."

Sara couldn't say anything else but couldn't contain herself either. Without another word she ran over and grabbed Shorty hugging him, holding on tight. At first surprised, not knowing how to react, he put his arms around her, the two of them standing there for a long time. My brothers and I stood by watching the exchange. All of a sudden we realized we had a rich black man workin the farm with us, at least rich as far as we knew. He must've been the richest black man in Mississippi. Junior shook his head back and forth with no expression on his face.

Wes asked, "Hey Shorty, could you buy me a horse?"

Junior smacked him on the back of the head saying, “Wes, you don’t ask somebody to buy you something, especially something as big as a horse.”

The rest of us had a laugh on Wes. Always a cut up, this time he fell right into it.

Sara found a widow lady to live with in Tupelo which cost a lot less than living at the college. After the first year, she got one of the few scholarships. Things began to get better with the economy after the war started in Europe. She found part-time work after class in Tupelo to help cover the rest of her expenses. My sister would be the only one of us to attend college. She has spent all her working years as a teacher. I’m sure she is a good one. All of us boys missed out on college for a number of reasons, most, but not all of which, were because of the upcoming war.

Hauling Logs

Over the next few years, all kind of things changed for us. After Sara graduated college she got married to a boy she met in Tupelo. Her fella went to college too, at Mississippi State, so she found somebody smart like herself. We had never known anybody who went to a big college like Mississippi State. They were married in the fall of 1941 right before the Japanese attacked our Navy at Pearl Harbor in Hawaii. None of us knew much of anything about an American Navy base called Pearl Harbor or an island called Hawaii. We certainly had no reason to know anything about the country of Japan.

The attack occurred in December, my junior year in high school. The newspapers had already been publishing plenty about problems the Japanese were causing for all their nearby island neighbors. They said our leaders in Washington could not let the United States stand by doing nothing. The war in Europe had been going strong for two years. The papers said England wanted our help, but President Roosevelt wanted to stay out if we could. After the Japanese attacked us though, he declared war on them and the Germans at the same time. People thought fighting a war on two sides of the world at the same time might be a big mistake, but our leaders decided we had little choice. Nineteen, and out of high school, Junior, with most of the boys over eighteen, joined the Army right after the President declared war. Mama didn't like the idea of him leaving to fight a war but understood once he made up his mind she had no chance of stopping him. He would insist based on principle which is how she wanted us to think, but this must have been scary to think about.

Junior left in April of 1942 for training in Missouri. Meanwhile, the President's CCC program entered its ninth year but had begun winding down. Every physically able young man over eighteen had left to fight in the war. Instead of building bridges or park lodges the country needed to build tanks and airplanes. The last of the CCC work in Mississippi had been scheduled for the summer of 1942. After we finished planting the cotton and school let out in May Uncle Wes found out the CCC needed help cutting timber for the buildup of Camp Shelby at Hattiesburg. The Army used the old World War I base for training new recruits for the new war. Uncle Wes told Shorty and me we could make pretty good money over the summer, but the work would be hard. This would be the last chance to earn any

CCC money. We scoffed at the hard work comment. Wes, fifteen, was too young to work for CCC. He stayed home to take care of our cotton. Shorty and I would be staying in a camp for about four weeks. Shorty, with many other older black men, had no problem getting this kind of work with such large numbers of young men of both colors gone into the Military.

The logging operation had already begun to cut mature loblolly pine trees from the forests around Hattiesburg before we arrived. Uncle Wes had been right about the work which lasted from early morning until dusk each day. Though the hours were no longer than we were accustomed to, the work itself required harder continuous physical labor. Shorty and I were assigned to load and haul logs from the woods to the site where they would be milled into lumber at Camp Shelby. The trees stood over fifty-feet high, some measuring more than twenty inches in diameter. After being cut down with the limbs removed, the lumberjacks sawed them into thirty-foot sections. Each section weighed over six-hundred pounds. A team of mules with a single man driving them dragged each log out of the woods to the loading site. A small crew of men would take over to load them on a wagon using two mules with a set of chains. The loaders first chained each log on both ends. Using more mules to pull the chains from the opposite side, each log rolled up over two others lying against the wagon, to fall onto the wagon. Loggers called the technique the cross-hauling method which could be pretty dangerous whenever a log got loose. We hauled up to eight wagon loads each day with each wagon holding twenty to thirty massive logs.

My job, called the 'Teamster,' required climbing on top of a loaded wagon to drive the load from the woods five miles to the milling location for off-loading. Nested together on top of each other with two heavy chains to keep them from shifting or rolling off the wagon, the logs laid precariously in place.

None of those logging jobs were particularly safe whether felling the trees, loading them, or hauling them away. Accidents of all kinds happened at least weekly. One week a lumberjack was crushed to death by a tree which got caught in the limbs of others while falling causing the cut tree to drop in an unexpected direction. The fellow didn't die right away. Someone gave him a cigarette while the men tried to figure out how to get the tree off him. He said smoking one more Camel would sure be nice before he died. As he finished his last smoke his eyes opened wide staring straight off into the woods before his head slumped to one side. Not able to witness any of it, those of us at the wagon loading area got the news from the men running back and forth into the forest either to look in on the tragedy or try to help. For the next few days at the camp, we didn't talk about much else. The unfortunate fella had a wife with two young kids at home. The man's fatal accident proved further to me how life wouldn't be fair to everyone all the time.

One rainy day, close to the end of our last week, I had a bad accident. We had worked out in a pouring rain all day long. Non-stop rain cooled things off but made walking around the loading site sloppy muddy. The wagon had cut deep ruts into the mud which the mules made worse as they struggled to move the loads. Logs became slippery to handle when wet. And slippery logs became difficult to hold in place with the bulky chains. Later in the afternoon, people were getting tired as were the animals. We loaded ten more logs on the wagon, each weighing over five hundred pounds. Loading went the same as all the other loads as did the tie down. But the wagon wheels dug into the mud requiring the mules a punishing amount of effort to get the load moving. We should have unloaded a log or two but didn't want to waste any time taking the chains off just to put them back on again. Everyone was ready to quit for the day. The mules tugged against their harness trying to obey the flicking from my whip. Either their continual jerking or else the wet logs created slack in the chains allowing them to come loose slipping off the load.

Someone yelled "chain break" while someone else yelled, "Jump Johnny."

Men scattered to get away from the wagon as the logs began rolling off down an embankment. My last memory was trying to jump down the hill to get clear, the load of logs bouncing along, following me to the ground.

Two weeks later at Baptist Hospital in Oxford, I regained consciousness. The doctors had me on morphine. Though the drugs helped somewhat with the pain, discerning between reality and dreams became a constant struggle. But someone sat next to my bed wearing an Army uniform. It was Junior.

"Hey Bud," he said. My brother sometimes called me Bud which must have been short for buddy.

"Hey, what happened?" My throat, dry from the drugs, made the words come out sounding scratchy and rough.

"Don't you remember any of it?"

"I remember someone yelling for me to jump but nothing else after that, what happened?" Every word uttered caused pain in my stomach.

"You went down a hill with a whole wagon load of logs. Shorty helped get them off you. They told Mama Shorty actually lifted two of those logs off by himself which sounds unbelievable, but that's what she heard."

"How long have I been here?"

"It happened a month ago. You've been in a coma ever since. Not a single doctor believed you could make it. I got here a couple of hours ago. When I told them about your accident my company CO pulled some strings to get me a week of leave before I get shipped out to California and on to the south Pacific. I'm goin to fight Japs Johnny."

"The Japs are in California? How did they get in?" I asked.

"No, I'll be in California, not the Japs. That's where we are leaving from. The medicine they're giving you has got you messed up. We're going to an island in the South Pacific to fight over there. I have to go back to San Francisco day after tomorrow. That's where our guys are heading out from."

Focusing almost solely on the pain, following any conversation took too much effort, "Why does my stomach hurt so bad?"

"The logs piled up on you with three landing across your stomach. The doctors said you don't have any skin or muscle there. But in a month or so, after you get stronger, they will take a piece of muscle from one of your thighs to replace what you had over your stomach. I'm not sure what they do about the skin. They said they've never had a case like yours. Sounds like they are going to try a couple of procedures they haven't tried before, but they've done a pretty good job of keepin you alive so far."

The idea of the doctors trying things on me they hadn't done before didn't seem good at all. Not feeling up to talking I must have passed out once or twice with him sitting there.

"How's Mama doin?" I asked.

"She's as good as she could be I guess. She sat right here in the room with you day and night the first two weeks. The doctors helped Sara convince her she needed to rest. She comes back about every other day though. Grandpa Eddie brings her. She said getting to see me for a short visit was the only good coming out of your accident. She's always looking for the good in things, huh? I told her you might not agree but would do anything to make her happy."

Though what he said had a good bit of truth in it, which made me laugh, laughing hurt too bad. Breathing hurt too bad. Lying still doing nothing hurt. Junior told me Shorty came to visit me every day or so. He said Shorty blamed himself for the accident, for not looking out for me better. Passing out again, nothing else from his visit stuck with me. Another two weeks went by before I woke up again. Shorty sat beside the bed holding my hand, his face calm, eyes closed. Though I couldn't hear anything his lips were moving, praying I suppose.

With my throat parched from lack of water or the effect of the drugs, I whispered in a gravelly voice, "Hey Shorty."

He looked up, tears beginning to fill his eyes saying, "I sure is glad to hear yer voice boy." He gave my hand a gentle squeeze.

"Where's Junior?" I asked.

"He's gone off back to fight the war. He lef yer mama near bout two weeks ago now. Miss Sara come down from Memphis to see him off to the train station at Holly Springs. They is pretty sad over him goin, but Miss Emilie, I mean yer mama, gave him a tiny Bible to take along. She tolt him it was up to God and hisself to keep him safe. She tolt him God would look after the big stuff but he had to look after the little stuff. I ain't sure what little stuff there is bout fightin a war, but yer mama always knows somethin the rest of us don't."

It took a minute to think through what he said. Mustering my best effort to smile, I said, "Maybe she means Junior has to watch out for the bullets flyin with God watchin out for whether or not he gets in the way of one. What do you mean Sara came to see him off? Is Sara still in college?"

Shorty reminded me Sara graduated long before my accident happened, got married, and moved to Memphis with her husband, Thomas, who had gone off to the west coast in the Navy a few weeks ago. The accident, the injury or the drugs made me forget lots of things, but forgetting my big brother had joined the Army wasn't one of them.

"How's Wes doin, helpin Mama out by himself?"

Shorty looked at the floor shaking his head. "Wes ain't there with Miss Emilie no more. He done run off and joined the Navy. That boy come into the barn one day sayin he had to go but couldn't stand to tell his mama. He said I would have to take care of her now. I'm doin the best I can. Yes siree, little Wes done lied bout his age to the Navy. He's no more than fifteen years ole. He's plenty big enough alright to pass for eighteen. Lots of boys is doin the same thing. Wes, he's got more spunk than brains in his head. But I'm mighty proud of him anyhow, truth be told."

It wasn't a stretch to believe Wes had gone in the Navy though remembering his age would have caused me to think otherwise. Difficult enough, at the time, to remember my own age, I had little chance of recalling Wes' or anybody else. The news of Mama having no one but Shorty to take care of her required some thought. He alone looking after her gave me no cause for concern whatsoever. If she could rely on anyone, she could rely on him. But the idea of all my siblings gone from our home troubled me. It felt like the beginning of the end of our family.

"You need anything you tell me, anything at all, but I gots to go get them nurses. They said if'n you wake up they wants to check in on you."

"I'm thirsty."

"I'll get them to fetch you some water; you jiss stay quiet and rest now." He smiled saying, "I sho is glad to see you awake boy. You had us all mighty worried, yes sir."

The next few weeks were spent sleeping and doing a lot of thinking, the sleeping fitful with the thinking foggy, both results of heavy doses of morphine. Too often, lying there at night staring at the ceiling, the single light bulb over my bed began to look like an apple. After a while the doctors wanted me to handle the pain with lower dosages of drugs. They said they didn't want me to get addicted. When they tried lowering the morphine dosage the pain became unbearable.

It seemed like every time I woke up Shorty sat there beside me. He told us stories my whole life but came up with new ones. He kept me informed on things too. Without him there day after day I may have gone out of my mind.

July went by, as did August and September. Later in October, the doctors said I might be strong enough to have the surgery removing muscle from my leg to use for my stomach. My hospital stay lasted a year. Obviously, my willpower proved the doctors wrong. There wasn't any part of "give up" in me. Being a Cook, we could be quite stubborn once we set our mind on something. The scars on the side of my right thigh resulting from the operation are an ever-present reminder of my short time hauling logs for the government. Finally, leaving the hospital the next summer, 1943, my entire senior year of high school had been spent in bed just trying to stay alive.

World War II Years

Somehow, when not visiting me, Shorty found time to tend the cotton crop. The war, creating more demand for cotton, pushed the price to double what it had been the last few years. Crop prices were higher than before the crash in 1929. Shorty hired another black fellow to help with the harvest. Spending his own money, Mama insisted on paying him back after harvest. She had the best year in a long time. Junior and Wes wrote letters home practically every day. Junior wrote from someplace in the Pacific on an island, but couldn't say where. Mama read in the papers how lots of our boys were stopping off in Australia for training before going into combat. She hoped he could stay there until the war ended though the experts in the news didn't foresee an end anytime soon. Wes was stationed in San Diego working in the supply depot. He wasn't happy staying safe in the states while the guys he trained with were heading out to sea on cruisers and battleships. Mama said she didn't care about his happiness, she wanted him someplace safe.

All of my male cousins joined or were drafted. The government lowered the draft age to eighteen. They were drafting anybody who wasn't over thirty-seven-years old. No more than a month after getting out of the hospital, just after my eighteenth birthday, my draft notice arrived. The government had no way of knowing who of us were fit to serve which required me to go to the courthouse at Holly Springs where they were signing high school graduates after a physical exam. A few were rejected for bad hearing or heart murmurs or any number of other problems. Many of the guys had no previous knowledge of the defects. The new skin on my stomach wouldn't be completely healed for several more months. A brace had been put across my mid-section to keep my insides intact while standing. The Army doctor asked me to take off the brace so he could examine the injury. Apparently, at first he didn't believe me, but after telling him I had to lie on my back before I could take off the brace the man shook his head saying something under his breath. Making some notes on my papers, he told me to go home, to get well. My papers said, 4F, which meant physically unfit for duty.

The following summer Shorty and I were busier than ever. With most of the other young men gone we had all the work we wanted. Grandpa Lewis was well into his seventies. All my uncles including Uncle Wes had their own families to take care of.

They all had to manage without the help of their boys. After we finished the work on our farm we would go to Grandpa Lewis'. We worked another few hours at his place most days until dark. We ate dinner together every night, sometimes at Grandpas. Of course, Grandpa Lewis would never allow a black person to eat inside his house. Informing him I would eat out in the back with Shorty didn't go over well. Grandpa didn't like my attitude on the subject, but Grandma made him keep his mouth shut. For as much as he believed in the old ways, she seemed to understand things were overdue for a change.

Some nights Mama saved beans, collard greens, and cornbread on the stove not knowing when we would come in. Shorty figured he must be in his mid-sixties but didn't know his own age for sure. But for being as old as he was the man never slowed down, working as hard as ever though he said he couldn't see as good in the last few years. Once in a while in the fall we went squirrel or rabbit hunting. He began to miss shots he never missed in the past. Observing him throughout the day Mama and I could tell his eyes were getting worse, but the man wasn't one to complain about anything.

The next year brought little change. Though we, with our European Allies, were making progress with the war in Europe, the situation in the Pacific continued to drag. Our troops were literally fighting from island to island winning more than losing, but every battle was costly. My brothers continued to write home several times each week. All of us wrote back often though admittedly letters from me to them were rare.

The tone of Junior's letters suggested an overwhelming desire for the fighting to end. Tired of it, like his buddies, he wanted to come home. The Japanese were losing ground slowly with their 'fight to the death' attitude. People lost brothers, sons, uncles, and fathers. Everyone dreaded the possibility of one day seeing a strange government vehicle pull into the driveway. Two men would get out of the car wearing military uniforms. They were usually accompanied by the family's preacher. No one ever got a visit for a soldier wounded in battle. The visitors always carried a telegram delivering the worst news to loved ones. With few words, the message was direct but respectful beginning with an apology. The balance of the telegram identified a son, or sometimes a daughter, and the date of the person's death, ending with the words Killed in Action. Women in the nursing corps stationed in dangerous places close to the fighting were killed sometimes.

The telegram Andrew Gurley's parents got reported him missing in action someplace in Belgium. Wondering about the fate of a loved one may have been worse than knowing for sure. Those poor folks wondered about him for the rest of their lives, but no news ever came. Word spread quickly when someone received bad news. The local paper would report the name a few days later. The government did a good job of hand delivering the horrible news before people would see it in the papers. People with loved ones in the service felt as though they were living out in the open under a thunderstorm all day every day. They hoped and prayed their family would be spared while waiting for lightning to strike in the form of a telegram.

With 1944 came the wettest spring we had in a long time which contributed to the crop being planted later than normal. Jane was old. Nursing a bone spur for quite a while she couldn't pull the plow. We borrowed a horse from Grandpa Lewis. He didn't mind us using his horse but said if we brought her back lame he would kick my "you know what." It didn't matter to him that I was a grown man. The old man would have made every attempt to make good on the threat. Persuading the borrowed horse to plow seemed to create more work than the plowing itself. She had an attitude worse than any mule which is saying a lot taking us until late May to get the cotton planted. Shorty, with all his skill handling mules, couldn't get Grandpa's mare to cooperate. At the end of planting, the lazy mare had no injuries, at least physically. More than happy to take her back to Grandpa Lewis, I hoped to never need use of her again.

June got hot. It stayed hot with barely enough rainfall to keep the young cotton seedlings alive. We heard stories of large plantations west of us, close to the Mississippi River, so dry the cotton struggled to break through the top layer of soil. Day after day Shorty and I worked side by side. We worked and talked. He would talk about anything. The man had answers for just about everything. Thinking back, some of them may not have been too accurate. A comment of some kind could be expected on virtually any topic. Sometimes for entertainment, I would ask something he could hardly know anything about just for the amusement of hearing what he had to say. One day it seemed appropriate timing to raise the subject from long ago about how his daddy died. He didn't know how much of the story I heard hiding behind the barn.

Leaving nothing out he told me the same as he had Grandpa Eddie but added for me, "Johnny, you got to make up yer mind what kind of man you is gonna be in this life. There ain't nobody who can decide for you. You boys has all growed up learnin the right things bout God and yer mama has done her best to teach you right from wrong. But it's up to you what you do once you go out in the worl. Most peoples try to do right but they's mean peoples everywhere. A lot of the mean ones don't know any better but that still don't make it right. If'n you grow up learnin the wrong things you're bound to do the wrong things lessen you can make up yer mind not to. It's hard to unlearn, but peoples can do it. I done it myself and I spect they ain't too many peoples can say they learnt or seen the kind of awful stuff I have. We is all jiss peoples Johnny, we is all the same on the inside. We jiss can't tell cause alls we can see is the outside." Speaking as we worked, he never looked up until finishing his last comment.

Nearly speechless I said, "Thanks, I promise you I'll do the best I can."

He didn't let the thought end there, "You don't have to promise me nothin boy, you make a promise to yerself and God. You don't owe me nothin, you don't owe nobody in this worl nothin. You don't ever owe no person that does somethin out of love. When a person cares bout you and does somethin it's a gift. You don't owe folks for a gift."

My nineteenth birthday had come in May. Like a typical nineteen-year-old, I had nothing else to learn. But this old, uneducated man proved me wrong again and again.

July began hotter than normal ending the same. August began the same way, but the humidity got so high the water couldn't stay in the air any longer bringing plenty of rain. The cotton needed both. It grew faster than a rabbit chased by a bobcat. Shorty and I got started early each day to work the fields before the heat could get too overwhelming. We took turns going back to the house late morning to bring leftover biscuits for a snack or get our water jar refilled. The biscuits could've just as well been taken along when we first went out in the morning to eat cold. But they were always better warm plus the short walk down the hill provided a break well worth the effort. We sat under a stand of pecan trees between two cotton fields to take our short rest one day the second week of the month. Shorty took his turn making the walk back. But not gone long enough to get all the way to the house he began calling me. Standing perfectly still squinting didn't help me hear any better until he got closer. He called my name as he hurried back up the hill.

Meeting him at the edge of the field Shorty stopped out of breath. Gathering himself, between breaths he said, "They's a govment car in front of the house. You gotta go to yer mama, right now."

Wasting no time to ask if he had a chance to go into the house or anything else I ran. We knew what the car meant. A black Plymouth sedan with a large white star on the front doors pulled away moving back to the main road as I reached the house.

Entering the back door I called, "Mama, Mama."

She didn't answer. Fresh cut tomatoes lay next to the knife she had been using at the kitchen table before the visitors arrived. She had taken an extra few seconds, probably after hearing a car pull up in the front, to take off her apron which lay crumpled, also on the table. The living room was dark. The front door had been left open with the screen door closed against any late morning mosquitoes. She sat beside the cold fireplace.

Stopping in the kitchen doorway I asked, "Mama, what is it, who came to the door?"

Still not answering she stared hard into the dark fireplace.

"Mama..." Beginning to ask the question I already knew the answer to she looked over, tears streaming down her face onto the paper in her lap.

"They've killed him, Johnny, they've killed my Junior."

There wasn't an ounce of strength in her, her right arm falling to one side she dropped the telegram to the floor. Crossing the room slowly and kneeling at her side I held her. She felt frail as if holding too tight could break her, trembling as my arms wrapped around her trying to offer comfort. My attempt to make her feel better in such a dark moment felt oddly absurd. Neither of us said anything for a long time, both crying, holding on to each other. At the time, no one else existed, nothing else mattered. Mama and I, at first, didn't notice Shorty come in. He stood in the kitchen doorway with tears running down his face.

After a while, Mama looked over to him saying, “Shorty, get me my Bible please.”

He answered somber and quiet, “Yes um.”

She never opened it though, saying nothing more for a long time holding the Bible in her lap with the telegram lying on top folded in half. We sat for more than an hour. Shorty never sat down as if standing guard duty over us protecting from any further evil to enter our presence. None of us got hungry the rest of the day. Mama asked me to go to Grandpa Lewis’. She said they needed to know right away. She said we could go to Grandpa Eddie’s in the morning.

Never in my life have I had to deliver worse news than telling my grandparents my brother was killed. Grandpa Lewis showed his sorrow shaking his head while staring saying nothing more than a quiet thank you for me bringing the news. Grandma Sara was distraught asking how Mama was doing. She had Grandpa drive her to our place right away. My brother was the only of their grandchildren who didn’t come back from the war.

Later in the evening I read the telegram. Like all the others we had heard about, the short note said nothing more than an apology, Junior’s full name, William B. Cook, the date he died, and a line at the end saying, ‘Killed in Action in the South Pacific.’

The telegrams were almost always followed with a letter from someone in the soldier's company, an officer or on occasion, other soldiers, buddies who fought alongside them. Mama didn't want to know anything more but allowed me to read them. Of course, they spoke well of his character saying he was a good soldier. They wouldn't write anything different about someone who died fighting with them though they were obviously telling the truth about my older brother. His unit had moved on which allowed them to give details of what happened. Apparently, they were fighting on an island called New Guinea close to Australia when the Japs tried to overrun them. We lost over four thousand of our own men in the battle but in the end were successful at taking control. My brother had been killed fighting for an unknown island in the Pacific Ocean against people we had no knowledge of a few years earlier. The Army took him with the other dead American soldiers to the Philippine Islands, burying them there at an American military cemetery.

Mama had nothing to say for days afterward, going about her routines, sitting quietly for long periods reading her Bible. Sara came to stay with us a week or two. We all had expected bad news since no letters arrived from him for the past two weeks. When his letters stopped coming we began to worry. Later on, the Army returned his personal effects, including his shaving kit. The small Bible Mama sent with him was tucked in the bottom of the box wrapped carefully in a piece of cloth. The Army returned his letters too. He had saved all the letters we sent. There were a few from Mama he never had a chance to open. Opening them later in life, long after Mama died, saddened me to read she had written saying she had no word from him for a while and hoped he was safe. Those letters were all postmarked in Mississippi after the day he died. She had kept writing him not knowing her son was already dead.

Memphis

After receiving the news about Junior, Mama never acted as if she cared about life. Her lifelong ability to find the good in everything seemed to have died with my brother. Some days were better than others, but something had changed, like a dark cloak of grief hanging around her shoulders. Rarely did she smile or do much of anything with a sense of pleasure or purpose.

Moving on took a long time as an admitted hatred for the Japanese people stayed inside me for years. I felt the Japanese were responsible for the war and my brother's death. Nothing Shorty taught me over the years about disliking people over differences could change how I felt. My hatred came out of what they did, not how they were different. Only time could heal the hurt.

Sometime the next spring Mama said she wanted to move to Memphis. The cotton crop, including the payout, had been good for the last few years. She had little need or interest in spending money. Grandpa Eddie helped her find a place east of downtown Memphis in an area returning soldiers were moving into. They either had wives or else soon married after returning which must have been difficult for her.

Having spent a good part of her life making and mending our clothes she found work as a seamstress at a laundry near her new place. Not wanting her to make the move alone, I had to go with her. We were leaving nothing of value behind. Grandpa Lewis never gave the farm to Daddy. Once Mama told me she wanted to move, I said she should sell the farm right away. She told me she didn't own a single acre. Apparently, Grandpa Lewis never signed the deed over to Daddy which didn't make sense prompting me to ask. The time had come for her to tell me the history between Grandpa Lewis and Grandpa Eddie.

She began, "The way I understand it when your Grandpa Lewis and my daddy were young men in their twenties something happened between them. All I know is what Daddy told me, but there's no reason to believe he would lie. Not once has my daddy ever lied to me. Grandpa Lewis had an old cur dog meaner than a snake. The dog followed him everywhere. Once while in Holly Springs his dog lit into a horse tied in front Watson's grocery store. Your Grandpa Eddie had just come out of the store. Standing on the front walk he saw the commotion thinking the dog might cause the horse to break loose. The horse could hurt somebody or itself. Daddy said the dog scared the horse to the point it began jumping all over the place so he tried to shoo the dog away, which only caused it to come after him. He landed a kick into the dog's rib cage knocking him on his side where he stayed trying to catch his breath. Your Grandpa Lewis didn't see any of the first part. He just saw my daddy kicking his dog. Daddy said he tried to explain, but Lewis wasn't having any of it. Nobody else saw any of it. The dog wasn't hurt bad, but since that day they won't bother to speak to each other."

"You mean all these years they've been mad at each other over a dog?" I asked.

Mama looked sheepish, a look unlike her. She had never seemed uncomfortable or uneasy talking about difficult subjects.

Before she could continue I said, "There's more, isn't there?"

After thinking a minute she began again, this time looking me in the eye, "Well, your Grandpa Lewis never wanted your daddy and me to get married. When we started seeing each other he told your daddy to stay away from those Daniels'. He wouldn't say why. It's likely because he realized his reason wasn't good. Your Grandpa Eddie told me the dog story. Your daddy got mad at your Grandpa Lewis telling him nothing or nobody would keep him away from me, including his own daddy, especially over a stupid dog. Lewis never forgave him for not listening. Later your daddy found out Grandpa

Lewis signed over the deeds on all the farms given to your uncles but never would for ours. Lewis said we could live here as long as we wanted but would never own the place. After your daddy died I expected Lewis to make us move out. Your Grandpa Lewis loves you children though. Maybe he wanted to wait until you all grew up and moved off before making me leave. That's one reason I want to go to Memphis now."

She must have read in my face the disbelief and resentment building adding, "But it's time for me to go anyway. You need to move on and get your own life started. I couldn't take care of this place if I did stay."

Thought through, she laid the long overdue story out as gently as she could. The revelation about my grandpa's lifelong feud left me angry. I loved Grandpa Lewis though often, through the years, his actions or comments about people made me uncomfortable. His toleration for black people seemed nothing more than a show because he would say things about them to Grandma Sara or my uncles. A smart man in plenty of other ways, Grandpa Lewis wasn't smart about people.

I asked, "What is Shorty supposed to do?"

Mama said, "I spoke to him already. I told him I intended to move, but he's a part of our family now and I wanted to know what he would do. He said not to worry, he has a sister living someplace in

Arkansas. She writes him on a regular basis and has told him many times over the years he could move in with her anytime he wanted or needed to."

With almost too much information to handle at once, my first inclination was to give Grandpa Lewis a piece of my mind, not concerned in the least how he would respond. A powerful man around our part of the state, Grandpa never heard anything negative from anybody, especially his own family. But the effect on Shorty of Mama and me moving troubled me more than anything. Moving away with her made sense but would require me to move away from my father. Shorty had become my surrogate father. Everything I learned about being a man came from him. The gentle soul took care of us for years. But the problem of Mama making the move to Memphis by herself had few good solutions. Sara lived there. Maybe she would be able to look after Mama. On the other hand, though, Mama was right. The time had come for me to find out what else life had in store. Rural northern Mississippi had little to offer and Mama wouldn't want me to stay with her long in Memphis.

Finding Shorty wasn't difficult. Like week after week, year after year since he first came to our place, the most likely place to find him would be the barn. There he was carrying the empty bucket just used to feed oats to our two mules. Too old to work, Jane would soon be sold for rendering. She never cared much for Pepper or other dogs for that matter. It seemed ironic she would end up as dog food. We bought a younger mule in time for planting season.

Finding the right words to start the conversation took me a while. “Hey Shorty how’s Jane doin today?”

He sensed right off my question about the old mule had nothing to do with the true reason for my intended conversation.

Playing along he said, “She’s right fine today, right fine for as ole as she is. How is you doin?” His delivery simple and subtle, Shorty had called me out as usual.

Having no reason to beat around it, I began but couldn’t get the words out without tearing up, “Mama said she talked to you about her moving to Memphis.”

Continuing with his work he shook his head once saying, “Yes siree, she tolt me bout you movin too.”

His response gutted me, concerned he might think I attempted to hide something. I felt lousy, worse than a traitor.

“I don’t have to move anywhere. Sara can look after Mama. You and me, we can work this farm together,” I said.

He stopped, turned to face me, standing with his hands to his sides, one holding a brush, the other a mule harness. His turn to say something had come, but what he said wasn't with words. The look he gave said all the man wanted me to hear.

Not willing to give in easily I said, "Why not? You want to stay here don't you?"

He answered, "Boy, I would stay with you til Jesus hisself comes again if'n I could have my way. But this ain't bout me, it's bout you. You go on up to Memphis and find yerself a life Johnny Cook. There ain't no life for you on this ole farm livin with a beat up ole mule and a half-blind ole black man."

Of course, he was right. He was always right which reminded me of Daddy. I was also reminded how often I threw Daddy in Shorty's face when he first came around. Any attempt at arguing with him now would be futile. The man standing in front of me meant everything to me. If he thought my time had come to move on, I would though it meant leaving him forever. It hit me though; Shorty had just referred to himself as black, a long forgotten difference between us.

I thought, 'Damn, why does life have to be so hard so often.'

Apparently able to read my mind too, he said, "It's a hard adventure this life, ain't it? Bout time we start carin bout somethin or somebody they goes away, or somethin bad happens to em. But it ain't jiss bout the hard times. Me and you, we got lots of good times to remember. I knows it and you knows it."

Taking a step toward me put an end to the matter. Closing the distance between us, we hugged each other as if somehow the gesture could prevent our loss.

We embraced a long moment before he pushed me gently away saying, “I’ll be up to my sister’s place in Pine Bluff. That’s no more than near bout one hundred-fifty mile from Memphis. I spect you’ll get yerself one of them Ford or Chevy sedans that’ll make the trip in no time. You better come see me when you can.”

The hardest moments over the years had always been made easier by his use of humor or changing the subject enough to minimize the problem at hand. A simple promise to visit as often as possible came up short of showing how much he meant to me.

After Mississippi

Wesley received his discharge from the Navy shortly after the war ended. Mama and I lived together for a while in a small house east of downtown Memphis. Once Wes came home we built a house for her. Shortly afterward, we built one for each of us. The cute girl living across the street from Mama found reasons to like me which are still a mystery. Wes and I found work at the Southern Railroad. Railroad work required long hours but paid well. Nothing would ever be as hard as plowing, chopping or picking cotton. There was a faint familiarity working for the railroad. Grandpa Eddie had done railroad work for over forty years before he retired. Though I never completely understood what his work was, being at the railroad gave me some kind of connection to him, a way of holding on to him.

Within a couple of years my brother and I were both married. The economy all over the country had taken off. The years of people struggling to find a job were over. We were having the best years of our lives.

The first year after the move to Memphis I went to visit Shorty a couple of times. His sister had a small farm which three grown sons helped her work. Her husband had died a few years earlier. Having Shorty around worked out well. He told me doing a full day's work had become harder, but his sister said he worked from dawn until dusk. Though admittedly putting in the hours, he said suggesting much got accomplished would be lying. One of her boys said Shorty did his best work on a bench behind their barn with his eyes closed.

Life continued to get more complicated for me. Business for the railroads grew tremendously with the rest of the economy. My bosses kept throwing opportunities in front of me requiring my growing family to move all over the southeast. A job in northwest Alabama a few years later would be the closest we ever got to Memphis and less than an hour drive to Holly Springs. We made the trip to Memphis once in a while to visit Mama, Sara' and Wes' families. I never found time for anything other than working and helping raise our family. Mama said Shorty's sister told her he had gone completely blind.

Ten years passed since my last visit. I had not kept my promise. A business trip took me to Memphis late one August. Finishing my business on a Friday gave me a chance to make the short trip to Pine Bluff the next morning. Turning off the highway, the county road to Shorty's sister's place was nothing more than a dirt road like those I knew growing up. The weather was hot. With the windows down and a cloud of dust trailing behind, the car pulled in stopping on the yard in front of the house. It was late afternoon. There he sat on the front porch. The long beard was whiter than any snow. He had a few tufts of hair on both sides of his bald head, also white as the cotton we had picked together. Well into his seventies he had on blue overalls covering a clean white shirt.

As I stepped from the car, Shorty spoke without looking my way, "It sure is a fine day today. And by the sound of it you is drivin a fine automobile. What brings you way out here?"

He stared into the distance holding his head up as if trying to smell something, unable to see anything. The sight of him and hearing his voice triggered a lifetime of memories. I couldn't move or think straight. Though anticipating our reunion on the entire drive over, at the moment a terrible feeling welled up inside me. My guilt instantly convinced me not keeping my promise to visit had somehow caused his blindness. As I took no more than a few steps toward the porch, he stood slowly out of his rocker. Turning toward me, staring off into the cotton field beyond he said, "Johnny. Is that you boy?"

I stopped literally in my tracks. "Yeah, it's me Shorty, it's me."

His face lit up, hardly visible through my own tears. His eyes were blind. My tears were blinding me. We clutched each other as we had all those years ago the afternoon he knocked the eight gauge from under my neck and years later when he told me to go make a life for myself. It took a few seconds before I could speak again. Here, bent slightly at the waist, holding on to me, stood the man who raised me, someone I loved more than almost any human alive. It dawned on me he wouldn't be able to see the pictures of my own boys, my daughter or my wife. I had waited too long.

It felt as if the sun had not risen or set a single time since we were last together. He said, "You gots to tell me bout that family I been hearin bout in yer mama's letters. My sister Rachel reads every one of em to me. Your mama's mighty proud of those grandchillren. Now you go get that other ole rocker over there and sit right here with me a spell."

I wanted to begin by apologizing for my total lack of communicating over the last years. "I'm sorry..."

He stopped me short placing the open palm of his hand against my lips. In a low voice but with assurance he said, "We ain't got time to talk no nonsense. I is an ole coot who ain't gettin no younger while you stand around here feelin bad for livin yer life. I spect you done lived a good one so far. I'd like to hear me some bout it if'n that's okay."

I'm sure he saw my smile though his eyes were clouded as solid white as a boiled egg. We sat for hours. Shorty wanted to know about my wife and each of my children, their names, ages, everything he could think to ask. The broad prideful smile left his face as he concentrated on listening close for the next several minutes.

At one point he said, "Which one of em is most like you?"

Knowing the question was loaded I asked, "In what way do you mean most like me?"

"You knows. I wants to know which one is the meanest and gets hisself in the mos trouble like his pappy used to."

His smile grew once more. He paused before adding, "And is the smartest and hardest workin."

The man couldn't allow himself to insult me long enough for me to play along. At some point late in the day, he stopped me in mid-sentence, looking at me with his white, blind stare to say, "Johnny Cook, I am most proud of you boy."

Responding would take all my courage. My adult life had been spent wondering what he would think of the life I had lived.

He added, "I'm plenty proud of all the things you done, but I'm mos happy for the kind of man you are. You a good man Johnny Cook, you done made me proud."

Nothing material in the world ever mattered to him. How people treated each other meant everything. Given his troubled background it would be understandable if what mattered more than anything centered on the issue of how white people treated blacks. But, his concern for justice never applied solely to one people group.

Some things require the right point of view to make a real difference. At the time, mine was as a father caring for my own children. Shorty admitting his pride in me felt as though it came from my own father. Receiving the one complement all grown children desire left me with nothing adequate to say. You lie in bed wondering, hoping before the end of your father's life he will acknowledge his pride, proof you are acceptable to him.

As a consequence of his affirmation it's as though you suddenly became acceptable to all of humanity, maybe to God as well. The coward in me wanted to look away though the old man could not see me cry. I didn't look away, but I did cry.

Rising from the rocker, I leaned in thanking him with another hug, his black hand patting me softly on the back as always. Rachel insisted I stay for a dinner filled with laughter and stories laced with a few tall tales. He had probably told the stories many times of the coon hunt or the little terrier who knew how to shake a bush. But he told them again over supper embellishing as any good storyteller would. His sister and nephews were a little surprised to have me vouch for every one of his stories.

Driving back across the Arkansas delta over miles of cotton fields, thousands of acres of cotton and soybeans, my mind filled with memories of the old days, the stubborn mule, squirrel hunting with Pepper, my two grandpas who were long dead and my brother Junior. Sadly, neither Daddy's face nor my older brother's would come to me. The years had caused my memories of them to diminish leaving nothing more than ill-defined moments of the time we lived through together. Life had been plenty difficult all those years ago, but now things were different. My new life was good, still hard at times but good, though maybe the old days were the best. While the sun set in the rearview mirror, seeing the road in front of me became quite demanding as my eyes filled with more tears.

Junior would have kidded with me saying something like, "Just turn on the windshield wipers, Bud."

A few more years went by. A phone call came from Wes. He said Shorty died in his sleep the night before. My boss gave me the next two days off. Picking Wes up in Memphis the next day around noon, we made the drive to Pine Bluff. We had a good visit driving over. They held Shorty's funeral at Grapevine Primitive Baptist Church. Wes and I were the only white people there. We introduced ourselves as Shorty's boys. That's who we were.

Funerals for old people are often poorly attended; I suppose because most of the people they knew are dead too. But many came to honor Shorty. The cemetery adjoining the small church held graves for people dating back to the Civil War. They were all black people. Realizing the older among them had been slaves added to my sorrow. And those who weren't slaves had lived during horrible times for them. A white picket fence surrounded the cemetery like every country cemetery I have ever been in, put there to keep the animals out or as a note to the living how special those places are. As they lowered him into the ground, the rain began, first a drizzle which soon became a steady downpour, not heavy, without wind or thunder, just constant.

The rain took me back forty years, standing in the cemetery at the Chewalla Baptist Church burying Daddy. The feeling came over me as if little Wes and I were burying him again, but Mama was gone now, Junior too. Looking away over my shoulder for a moment to the white fence I fully expected and hoped in my heart to see a short round black man standing with a soaked hat in his hands, but he wasn't there. Shorty was nowhere to be seen. His time was over, but for my family, the man will never be completely gone, nor his time completely over. As rain mixed with tears streamed down my face, I squinted, craning my neck, looking hard for him. Knowing in my head he would not be there didn't matter. My heart wanted one more glimpse back into the past, our past.

Standing next to my brother in the rain I made Shorty one final promise. Working hard to keep it over the years, I committed to treat other people the way he taught me promising to teach my children to do the same. As the tears slowed I looked around. Few people had left, but I no longer saw any black people. They were merely people, like Shorty.

ROSE MOUNTAIN

by: William D. Bramlett

Coming in 2019

Watch for this story of three young Americans tasked with destroying Adolf Hitler's nuclear weapon. A formidable Belgian Major attempts to help their cause as they cross Europe, infiltrating the heart of Hitler's weapons team, pursued by a ruthless and capable German Officer.

The characters exhibit honor, sacrifice, courage, and loyalty, as they come to life affected by the realities of war while facing the consequences of failure.

Made in the USA
San Bernardino, CA
14 December 2018